L ONG LONG AGO two sisters, Maria and Amelia, grew up in a tall narrow house.

They started a school and did quite well.

Then one dark winter's day, there came a new pupil, Sara Crewe.

And her story was the story of A LITTLE PRINCESS ...

      very rich ...

            ... then poor.

In the attic with a rat ...
    ... but then came sparrows on the roof,
        cherry cake for a secret party with friends ...

        ... and *magic*.

And then she went away, and was happy ...

Except, she left her best friend Ermengarde behind ...
    and the rat ... and the sparrows
        ... and all the other girls too.

    They had to carry on the story without her ...

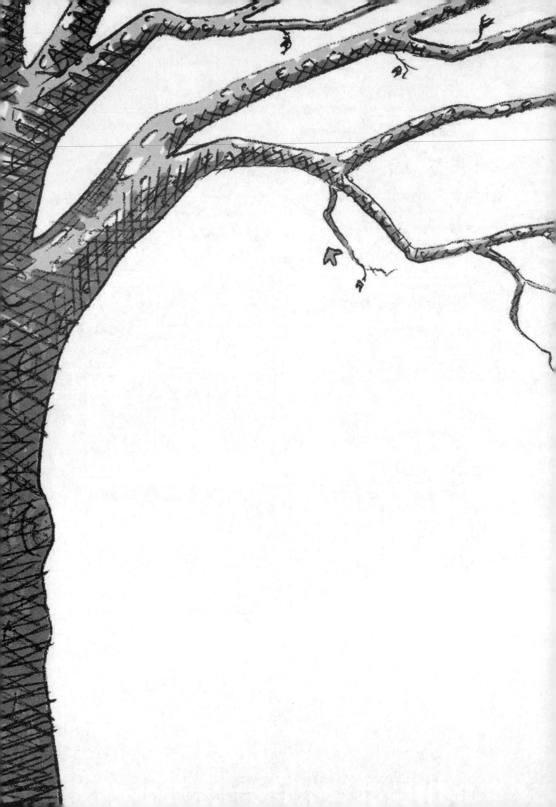

Wishing for Tomorrow

HILARY McKAY

Illustrated by Nick Maland

Hodder
Children's
Books

*To my father, who always loved to tell stories
to children, with love*

Author's note

The hundred-year-old story of *A Little Princess* has fascinated me for many years. As a child, I read and reread it, mesmerised by the world it described; early twentieth-century London, an old-fashioned school, rainy pavements and candlelit attics, the smell of hot currant buns to a hungry child, the rustle of rose-coloured silk. I knew the details so well I could have lived there myself. There was a transformation scene that was pure magic, a villainous headmistress, a mysterious benefactor, a scullery maid, a flock of girls, a little princess, and (of course) a perfect ending. Perfect, that is, in all respects but one.

Because when Sara the little princess drove away with the mysterious benefactor and the scullery maid, the rest of us did not go with her. We were left behind, exactly where we had been before she arrived.

That could not have been the whole of it! Surely Lottie and Lavinia, Ermengarde and all the rest of that seething bunch of opinions did not just fade into the shadows. Did they not have a story too? What happened next?

That was the question I asked as a child, and a generation later when my daughter read the story in her turn, she asked it too.

And so I have written the answer.

Here are Lottie and Lavinia, Ermengarde and all the rest, stepping back from the shadows and into the light. This is the story of what happened next, after Sara went away.

Ermengarde's Birthday
(Part One)

ONCE UPON A TIME THERE WAS A CITY.

In the city there was a square.

In the square there was a house.

It belonged to two sisters, Miss Maria Minchin and Miss Amelia Minchin.

From the street the house looked very much like all the other houses in the square. Tall and narrow and respectable with servants in the basement, faces at the windows, and sparrows on the roof. If anything made it a little different from its neighbours it was the faces at the windows. There were so many of them, and they looked out so often, and they were all girls. There were little girls, bouncing up to wave to anybody passing in the road below. There were big girls, telling secrets and using the windowpane reflections to admire their hair. (Mirrors were very rare in the Miss Minchins' house, and the few that existed had such thick cheap glass that even the prettiest, healthiest people looked like they had been recently drowned in green water.)

And as well as the little girls and the big girls there was Ermengarde, who was too shy to wave, and never told secrets or admired her reflection (having been brought up to believe she was plain). Ermengarde gazed out of the windows more than anyone, and her eyes were always wide and expectant, as if she was waiting for the answer to a question, or the end of a story. Sometimes she pressed so close to the glass that her nose turned into a flat white blob and her hands became two splayed pink stars. Mostly, however, she just sat, while the others talked around her. Sometimes she didn't even listen.

Eight-year-old Lottie always listened.

Lottie was officially a little one, but it was the school's older students who interested her most. Lavinia, for instance, an unpredictable girl with a sharp and lovely face, and a way of glancing through half-closed eyes that even her best friend Jessica sometimes found slightly scary.

Lavinia was the most interesting girl in the school, decided Lottie. Jessica was the prettiest. Gertrude was the rudest. Ermengarde . . .

'Ermengarde is a nonentity,' said Lavinia.

'She *is* a plod,' agreed Jessica, and it was true that Ermengarde did not shine at anything, not lessons, nor games, nor jokes, nor stories round the fire. She had one skill however: she was very quick and deft at freeing insects that were trapped against the glass.

'Once there was a butterfly,' said Lottie. 'A big dark butterfly with yellow edges on its wings. But it is usually just bluebottles . . .'

'Disgusting things,' said Lavinia.

'. . . or wasps.'

'I'm sure you're supposed to *kill* wasps,' said Jessie.

Ermengarde never took any notice of these remarks. It was something she loved to do, to release the desperate buzzing into an airy silence. She would have released all the faces at the windows too, if she could, even including the stinging Lavinia.

Ermengarde did not think the Miss Minchins' house was a good place to be.

The house was a school, a boarding school for girls. It was full of whispers. The whispers were part of the pattern of the house, like the peculiar musty smell from the basement (part dinner, part dampness), the tick of the enormous grandfather clock in the hall, the nightlights that burned in their saucers of water, and the scratchings and squabblings of the sparrows on the roof.

Often the whispers came from behind the curtains, sometimes several voices, fluttering and chattering.

Diamond mines!

Her French is perfect!

I guessed that Becky was under the table!

Once (at a high window without curtains) it was just one voice, very quietly:

My papa is dead.

Ermengarde, staring intently into the bare branches of the plane trees outside, on the afternoon of her thirteenth birthday, whispered,

I thought we were best friends.

'What did you say, Ermie?' asked Jessica, overhearing.

'I was talking to myself.'

'That's a sign of madness,' said Jessica, che 'isn't, it, Lavvie?'

'Not that I've heard,' said Lavinia, so coldly that Jessica backed away and joined Ermengarde at the window instead.

'Fancy crying on your birthday!'

'I am NOT crying,' snapped Ermengarde. 'Go AWAY and leave me ALONE.'

Jessica did not do either of these things. Instead she waved across the square at a passing cab, flicked her curls and asked, 'Are you actually completely thirteen yet? Do you know the time that you were born? I was born at five minutes to midnight on a beautiful starry warm night.'

'You can't possibly remember the *weather*!' said Ermengarde.

Jessica groaned.

'And I don't believe you could tell the time either,' continued Ermengarde. 'Not new born.'

Jessica said that of course she hadn't remembered the weather, or told the time, her mamma had done those things and recounted them to her as part of the story of the miracle of Jessica's birth.

Ermengarde sniffed and looked more miserable than ever, and too late Jessica recalled that Ermengarde did not have a mamma. Before she could think of any tactful comment to make on this sad fact, she was interrupted by Miss Amelia, hurrying into the schoolroom to inform Ermengarde that the carrier had just arrived with a package.

'From your Aunt Eliza, dear,' she said, panting a little.

'Oh,' said Ermengarde.

'*Isn't* that nice?'

'Yes, thank you.'

'Look *pleased*, Ermie!' said Jessica, as Ermengarde got up very slowly from the window seat and plodded after Miss Amelia towards the door. 'It's probably something special for tea! Wasn't it your Aunt Eliza who sent that great big . . . *OUCH! Lavvie!* That hurt!'

'It broke my pen too,' said Lavinia, inspecting the weapon with which she had jabbed her friend.

'I was only going to ask if it wasn't her Aunt Eliza who sent that great big hamper last term,' said Jessie.

'I know you were.'

'You've made a scratch on my arm! It's nearly

bleeding! I may get blood poisoning! *Look* at it, Lavvie!'

'Dear me,' said Lavinia, not looking.

'You might at least say sorry!'

'Shut up, Jess, and go and find me a new nib!'

Jessica went, only slightly outraged, partly because she usually did do as Lavinia ordered, partly in the hope of getting a glimpse of Ermengarde's parcel, but mostly because she was terribly bored. It was a very dull afternoon, in a very dull term, quite unlike the previous one when there had been excitements almost every day.

'Who would have thought,' she said to Ermengarde, who was in the hall picking at her parcel in a very gloomy kind of way, 'that after all that fuss we had before Christmas everything would just fizzle out! And be exactly the same as it was before.'

'Nothing is the same as it was before,' said Ermengarde.

The parcel was a birthday cake. It was so large that it was given a little table of its own in the dining room. It had pink and white sugar icing with a pink sugar rose in the centre, and green sugar writing curling around the edge:

Ermengarde Thirteen Years

Lottie looked at it with interest and asked, 'How do they make the letters green?'

'Snake juice,' said Lavinia.

'Lavinia!' said Miss Amelia. 'Ermengarde, please don't scowl like that! Lavinia was just making a little joke!'

'The pink is beetle juice,' said Lavinia calmly, 'and the green is snake. I hope.'

'Really, Lavinia!' scolded Miss Amelia. 'Ermengarde! Please be careful with that knife! Do stand *still*, Lottie! You are bumping people! Come, Ermengarde! Cut your cake, dear!'

'And you must make a wish as you cut, musn't she, Miss Amelia?' added Jessie.

'Well, if she would like to,' agreed Miss Amelia, smiling a little nervously, as she always did when forced to make a decision.

Ermengarde looked around the room, greenish walls, greenish gas light brackets and heavy greenish curtains. And then she looked at the faces at the table, some snuffly with colds, some pinched, some round, some bored, some eager.

No smiles.

'Hurry *up*, Ermie!' begged Lottie.

'She is thinking of her wish,' said Jessica.

'Perhaps she has no wish,' suggested Lavinia. 'Perhaps her life is perfectly perfect, like a little princess's.'

This unkind remark stung Ermengarde into speaking at last.

'My life is *not* perfect. It is not a *bit* perfect,' she snapped. 'And I *do* have a wish, so there, Lavinia!'

'Wish it!' ordered Lottie.

'I will,' said Ermengarde, and she gripped the knife and stabbed hard through the heart of the sugar rose and heavy and deep into the cake's plump, jammy centre, and she said, 'I wish . . . I WISH AND WISH . . . *I WISH AND WISH AND WISH* . . . that there was NO Miss Minchin's!'

'*Ermengarde!*' exclaimed Miss Amelia.

'Well, I do,' said Ermengarde, and burst into tears.

Later she was persuaded to eat a piece of birthday cake by Lottie, who brought a fat slice to where she was sitting being dismal by a black and rainy window.

'I expect it's only grass juice that makes the letters green,' said Lottie, as comfortingly as she could. 'Or cabbage. I'm afraid the pink really is beetle, though. Miss

Amelia said so. But it can't be a poisonous sort of beetle because we've all eaten it and we are still well.'

Ermengarde sniffed.

'Anyway,' said Lottie. 'I've brought you a birthday present.'

Lottie's parcel contained a green tin frog with a key in its back. It played a small tune when it was wound, and opened and closed its mouth to show a black painted fly.

'Thank you,' Ermengarde said, and added rather mournfully, 'It's my best present. Thank you.'

'What else did you have? What did Sara send?'

'A book. I don't know why. She knows I hate books. And my godmother sent mittens. She always sends mittens,' said Ermengarde ungratefully. 'Aunt Margaret sent a prayer in a picture and my papa sent a gold sovereign that he hopes I will use for something sensible. And Aunt Eliza sent the cake.'

'You've got my frog now though,' said Lottie, complacently. 'And your birthday wish. And one day it will come true.'

'How do you know?'

'Lavinia said.'

'*Lavinia?*'

'Lavinia said one day in about a million years all the planets and this whole world and England and London and Miss Minchin's will be swallowed up into the sun. Gulp! Bang! And that will be the end.'

Lottie appeared to find this idea very attractive. She hugged herself with pleasure, slid off the window seat and settled into a cheerful squabble with a fellow eight-year-old over the few remaining petals of the sugar rose.

Ermengarde nibbled her cake and wound up her frog and was a tiny bit consoled. It was nice to know that there was a definite end to Miss Minchin's in prospect, even if it was some time away.

2

Miss Minchin's

MISS MINCHIN SELECT SEMINARY FOR
Young Ladies, read the brass plate by the door.

The brass plate was less shiny than it once had been.
Just before Christmas, Becky, the scullery maid, had
gone away, and her reverent polishing was now a thing
of the past. The new maid's polishing was frequently no
more than a good spit and a rub with the corner of her
apron as she went by.

The brass plate was less shiny, and the Select
Seminary was . . .'Less Select,' admitted Miss Amelia,
younger sister of the headmistress, plump and harassed
and outnumbered by girls. Fourteen girls altogether,
eight little, six big.

'Only fourteen,' Miss Amelia had said worriedly after Christmas. 'Still, just now, with poor Maria as she is. . .'

Maria was Miss Minchin. In the days when the brass plate had sparkled like a jewel she had been a power that left Miss Amelia limp and breathless. Lately, however, a strange thing had happened. Somehow, in Miss Amelia's mind, she had become poor Maria.

'Although perhaps in a way she always *was* poor Maria,' said Miss Amelia to herself. Among her day-to-day fluster of worries and fusses and gasps, Miss Amelia sometimes had surprisingly sensible thoughts.

'Yes, perhaps she was. Poor Maria,' repeated Miss Amelia, and her memory began to travel back through the years to the long ago time when they were not yet the Miss Minchins of the Select Seminary. To the time when they were Maria and Amelia, eldest and youngest children in a family of two girls and two boys.

Maria had been a difficult child. Large-boned, intelligent, always tormenting her parents with questions. 'Why must only the boys learn Latin? Ride in the park? Visit the museums? Why must the boys have new suits *again*?' And most often of all, '*Why* are things so unfair? *Why* was I born a girl?'

Poor Maria grew into a most unsatisfactory young lady. Her bones were larger than ever, she was definitely and hopelessly plain, and she was prone to nightmares that she would never describe.

She was very hard to live with. Her parents avoided her as best they could, but Amelia and the boys seemed never to escape.

'There is *nothing nice* about Maria,' her brothers complained one miserable Christmas, and Maria heard.

'She was crying,' whispered Amelia, horrified. 'I think she was crying.'

'Maria,' said the boys, 'does not cry.'

'It *sounded* like crying.'

The boys said they didn't believe it, and they were probably right. Maria never did seem to cry. A few years later when her brothers died within weeks of each other, one in a riding accident, the other (mysteriously) in Italy of an unknown disease, the rest of the household was sodden with grief, but Maria did not shed a tear.

By that time she was definitely an old maid and Amelia was grown up.

'What a *waste*!' lamented Maria, at the second funeral.

'All they had! Schools! Oxford! Travel! All that money! Wasted!'

'Oh Maria, don't say that!' begged Amelia.

'Wasted!' repeated Maria. 'And who is to take care of Father and Mother if you marry, Amelia? Me, I suppose!'

Amelia did not marry, although she thought of it often. Father and Mother died soon after their boys, solving that problem, but as soon as it was over another appeared.

'Where has all the money gone?' cried poor Maria. 'Stop *wailing*, Amelia! How can I think, if you wail?'

Maria did manage to think however, she thought of a school.

'A school?' asked Amelia. 'Us?'

'Well, there is no one else!'

'But,' protested Amelia, 'but we know nothing about teaching! What could we teach?'

'We will teach,' said Maria sweepingly, 'everything! There is no point in doing things by halves! And there is no need to look so aghast, Amelia! I will naturally take charge. You need only do as you are told.'

And that was how the school began, with Miss Amelia

doing as she was told, and Maria in charge and brimming with schemes and plans.

'We will keep it very select,' she decided. 'We will specialise!'

'Specialise?' enquired her sister.

'We will specialise,' pronounced Maria, magically inspired with a truly wonderful idea, 'with pupils whose parents are . . . detached!'

'*Detached?*'

'Uninterested. Think about it, Amelia! There must be thousands of girls who simply do not interest their parents,' said Maria, who certainly knew, having been one herself. 'Or parents who, if not uninterested, are absent. Abroad. Or very ill . . . We may even take in girls with a mother or father who are . . .'

'In prison?' ventured Amelia, horrified and excited all at once.

'Certainly not! Good heavens, Amelia! Have you no sense at all? Dead, I was about to say. Dead!'

Amelia saw a difficulty, which was the problem of advertising for pupils with parents who were detached, abroad, uninterested or dead.

'However we word it,' she complained, 'It is

going to sound odd.'

Maria sighed. 'We will not advertise it as such,' she said. 'We will simply offer provision for holidays, as well as term time. It will come to exactly the same thing.'

She was quite right: it did. And so the Select Seminary began, in the dark London house that had been the home of the Minchin girls. It was one of a row of houses overlooking a scrubby square of railed London grass, plane trees and privet. The church was an easy walk away, there were hotels close by ('For visiting relatives,' said Miss Minchin, 'supposing any should wish to visit,') and there was a doctor just across the square ('Should any parents be deterred by the thought of sending delicate children away from home,' explained Miss Minchin).

They had good luck from the start; detached parents handed over their daughters and cheerfully paid extra holiday fees, rather than bring them home again. Miss Amelia received pocket money for the first time in her life. Miss Minchin's bony smile grew wider, her nightmares stopped, and she bought herself a gold locket on a long gold chain, something she had wanted since childhood. Anyone who looked inside would have found that it was empty, but of course no one ever did.

The Seminary flourished so well that one summer Miss Minchin actually abandoned the younger children to Miss Amelia and took her six eldest pupils to France.

Miss Amelia ran amok in that first freedom of her life. She attended church three times every Sunday, bought a hat trimmed with cornflowers and poppies that she hardly dared look at once it was in place, and became so breathless that it was quite a relief when Miss Minchin came home to squash her back to normal again.

'Paris was somewhat bleak,' reported Miss Minchin upon her return, astonishing Miss Amelia, who had heard many good and bad reports about Paris, but never that it was bleak. 'But the hotel was very pleasant. Very obliging. They somehow had the impression that I was Distantly Related . . .'

'Distantly related to whom, dear?' asked Amelia, after trying in vain to recall any Parisian Minchins that she had somehow overlooked.

'Oh, really, Amelia!' snapped Miss Minchin. 'You know perfectly well how everybody used to comment on your likeness to Our Beloved Victoria . . .'

'Maria!'

'I simply mentioned to someone that my younger sister looked far more like her than I. And you know what the French are like about royalty . . .'

'La Guillotine,' murmured Miss Amelia.

'*No!* Amelia, not for years now! Quite the reverse!'

So on the whole the French visit was a success, the bleakness of Paris being forgiven for the deliciousness of being thought even slightly of royal blood.

'Something may come of it,' said Miss Minchin, dreaming of princesses, 'and the whole thing is certainly a subject worth mentioning to parents.'

So it was. '*My Time in Europe*' sounded very impressive. It impressed people who should have known better, like Mr St John, Ermengarde's father, who had travelled in Europe for years, spoke seven or eight languages in consequence, and imagined Miss Minchin did the same.

It also impressed Lady Meredith, who impressed Captain Crewe, who was the father of a rich little girl named Sara Crewe.

Sara came to the seminary, enchanted Ermengarde,

made friends with the scullery maid and enemies with Lavinia,

'And ruined everything,' said Miss Minchin.

3

The Beginning of the Story

HOW DID SARA RUIN EVERYTHING?
wondered Miss Amelia. When did it begin? How did
everything change?

For years and years nothing had changed. There were
girls and there were lessons. There were walks round the
square and homesick tears. There were anonymous dull
servants, dull rooms and dull meals. Summer brought
white dresses, stifling bedrooms, lilac and flies. Winter
was chilblains and snuffles, damp woollen coats and a
fire in the schoolroom.

Stories laced the years together. Some lasted for
hours, and some for weeks. They smouldered, burned,
swept through the house and faded away as the

next one took over.

The latest story, Ermengarde's story, had begun the previous November, in the attic.

It was night-time, and it was cold, and Ermengarde was in the attic, where she should not have been. She was supposed to be in bed, but the attic was Sara's place, and Ermengarde was Sara's friend and there was nowhere else that they could meet.

At the Miss Minchins' house the attic was where the youngest servants slept, which meant Becky, the forlorn little scullery maid, and Sara, who was part kitchen maid and errand runner, and part teacher and helper with the little ones.

It had not always been like that for Sara. Once she had been the richest pupil in the school, so special that she had been treated like a little princess.

Sara's father, much to the admiration of most of the Select Seminary, had invested his fortune in diamond mines.

'Oh, very nice!' Lavinia had commented when she heard this news. 'Let us hope they are full of diamonds then! Unless he and Sara are particularly fond of very deep holes in the ground.'

Nobody took much notice of this remark. No one else at Miss Minchin's, not even Miss Minchin herself, could imagine a diamond mine that was not full of diamonds. They were all dreadfully shocked when the fortune was lost, and Sara's father died and Sara herself was discovered to own nothing except (as Lavinia had once rather hoped) some very deep (empty) holes in the ground.

'It can't be true!' wailed Ermengarde, but it was true and Sara had disappeared into another world. She left her friends in the schoolroom and began a remote new life, working all day, and spending her nights in a bare little room high up under the tiles.

Then for a long time her friendship with Ermengarde had seemed to end.

End? Ermengarde had wondered. I cannot bear it to end!

Long ago, when Ermengarde was only seven years old she had bravely approached Sara and asked if they could be friends. After Sara moved to the attic she had been forced to be brave for a second time, and to make friends all over again. That was how she came to know the secret world where Sara lived, with Becky in the room next door, and the sparrows on the roof for company.

'I like the sparrows,' Ermengarde, had said once. 'But this attic is a strange place, Sara. There are so many shadows, and it is terribly close to the sky. I get dizzy looking up. I feel like I might suddenly whoosh out of the skylight.'

They had laughed together then, and climbed on to Sara's old wooden table to watch the sunset and feed crumbs to the sparrows, and they had been happy.

However, the attic was not often a happy place, and on this particular November evening, when Miss Minchin had been scolding on the stairs, and Becky was sobbing into her pillow in the room next door, Ermengarde realised that it could be dreadful.

This was because she had just discovered that Sara, princess Sara, Sara whom no rags nor hard work could turn into a scullery maid, Sara her dear friend, was hungry.

Not hungry in the way that you become during the Sunday sermon in church, wondering which pudding will follow the roast beef. Nor the sudden emptiness caused by the smell of a warm baker's shop on a cold morning.

A different, awful kind of hunger.

If Ermengarde had ever before met someone who felt like that, she had not known. It was such an awful shock that for a minute or two she could not think. And then all at once she had realised that there was something she could do.

'Something splendid!' she had exclaimed, and her face was suddenly so bright and awake that she did not look like the usual Ermengarde at all.

That morning she had received a hamper, sent by her Aunt Eliza. It was the hamper that Jessica was to remember the following term, long after Sara had gone.

That was how the secret party had begun.

As soon as she remembered the hamper Ermengarde had no thought of waiting. It must be fetched at once, she had decided. Becky was crying, and Sara was faint with hunger.

They need it *now*, thought Ermengarde, as (quaking with nervousness) she tiptoed downstairs.

A few minutes later, laden and triumphant, she had returned to her friends.

'I'll tell you what, Sara,' she had said, inspired by a

sudden and brilliant thought. 'Pretend you are a princess again and this is a royal feast.'

It had been a miserable hungry day for Becky and Sara, and a miserable lonely one for Ermengarde. No feast was ever more needed, nor more gladly given.

'It will be a banquet!' said Sara.

It was a very well supplied banquet. The hamper that Ermengarde had carried up to the attic was meant to last her for weeks.

'*Wonderful* Aunt Eliza!' Ermengarde had rejoiced at the sweets and oranges and figs, currant wine, chocolate, jam tarts and little pies. And cherry cake.

They began with cherry cake. They each had a slice in their hands when they heard the footsteps on the stairs.

Ermengarde began to tremble.

Footsteps on the attic stairs, a heavy bang on the attic door, and the hard voice of Miss Minchin, headmistress of the school, destroyer of banquets, tormenter of little girls, tyrant of servants, victim of nightmares and rages and terrible pains in the side of her head.

'So Lavinia was telling the truth,' said Miss Minchin, and all the rose-coloured magic vanished into greyness.

* * *

Becky had been slapped and sent to bed in disgrace. Sara had been condemned to a day without food. The banquet had been seized. Ermengarde had been marched away, scolded until she wept, and shut in her room.

'Say your prayers!' ordered Miss Minchin when she left her alone at last.

For a long time Ermengarde had sat huddled on her bed, her tears all gone, her thoughts all with her friends. She tried to say her prayers, but got stuck on the line 'Give us this day our daily bread'.

'*Give them their daily bread*,' she prayed. '*Sara and Becky. And give them lots with butter and give them dinners and puddings and milk. And if you do I will forgive Miss Minchin the trespass she did against me . . .*

'*I suppose . . .*' said Ermengarde, very begrudgingly.

'*. . . For thine is the Kingdom*,' she continued, tactfully skipping the part about being delivered from evil, which plainly had not happened. '*The power and the glory . . . Haven't you seen how thin Sara has got? You look, next time she feeds the sparrows.*'

Ermengarde crawled into bed and pulled her red shawl

tightly around herself. '*For ever and ever* ...' she murmured, yawning. '*That sounds like a story* ...'

And then she was asleep.

4

In the Schoolroom

ERMENGARDE'S PUNISHMENT HAD LASTED
a week, and after that she was back in the schoolroom
again. At first she had worried that Miss Minchin would
send Sara away, but by the end of the week she knew
that she was still in the house. Several times she had
caught glimpses of her, although they had never had a
chance to speak.

Becky was also still there. Ermengarde, still in exile
from the schoolroom and struggling through her
arithmetic in the parlour one morning, had jumped at
the sound of a very loud crash. It was followed by the
voice of Miss Amelia scolding outside the door. Becky,
it seemed, had accidentally dropped a scuttleful of coal

in the middle of the usually immaculate entrance hall.

'You were *swinging* it,' complained Miss Amelia.

'Yes, mum,' agreed Becky. 'It was silly. I didn't oughter have. I'm picking it all up and I'll get a brush for the dust.'

'Well, do it quickly!' ordered Miss Amelia. 'What ever will it look like if someone comes to the door! Call Sara to help you!'

Oh! thought Ermengarde. Perhaps now I will have a chance to speak to them!

She had jumped up and tiptoed to the door in time to hear Sara arrive and exclaim, 'Goodness, Becky!'

'I was doing a twirl,' Becky explained. 'I came over really happy, Miss, all of a sudden, and the coal flew out of my hand!'

'Becky!' Ermengarde heard Sara say in an agonised whisper. 'That was so silly! You *must* be more careful! You must behave as if things were just the same as always! I couldn't *bear* it if . . .'

Then Miss Minchin's footsteps came tapping out from the schoolroom and Ermengarde stole back to her seat and did not hear any more. But she wondered. Sara had sounded truly frightened. What was it that she could not bear? If Becky should be sent away?

That must be it, Ermengarde had supposed.

Miss Minchin's pupils were divided into two distinct groups, the big girls and the little ones.

Lavinia led the big girls. Before Sara had arrived she had been the school's star pupil. She had resented Sara taking that place, and rejoiced when she lost it. Lottie once said that Lavinia would grow up into a witch. Ermengarde could imagine that, a very pretty witch, with pale blonde curls and a sharp little nose. Jessie and Gertrude, her best friends, could be the two tame cats who watched her spells.

Lottie was a different kind of leader, stubborn and unsquashable with a very strong tendency to always do exactly as she liked. It was Lottie who bounced up to Ermengarde on the first day of her reappearance in the schoolroom to tell what had finally happened to Aunt Eliza's hamper.

'Miss Minchin gave it to Miss Amelia,' she explained. 'And Miss Amelia gave it to us. The big girls wouldn't eat it. They said everything was too crumby and tumbled about, but the rest of us did and it was lovely. It would just have been thrown away if we hadn't. Do you mind?'

'Not really.'

'I saved an orange and some chocolate for Sara.'

'Oh, Lottie, did you? That was clever!'

'Yes, but she wouldn't take it. She was afraid Miss Minchin wouldn't like it, she said.'

'Poor Sara,' said Ermengarde mournfully.

'Yes, but she's all right, Ermengarde.'

'How do you know that?'

'I asked her,' said Lottie cheerfully. 'When she was taking our French lesson. I said, "Es-tu all right, Sara?" and she said, "Chut! Lottie, mais oui, merci beaucoup!" That means yes and be quiet,' Lottie kindly translated.

'I'd rather speak to Sara in English,' said Ermengarde. 'I will, as soon as I get a chance.'

A day or two later she had managed it. It had been a particularly nasty afternoon, ending in an early-evening visit by her father. 'I discovered I had an hour to spare before my train,' he had explained. 'Your Aunt Eliza sent you this rug, by the way, she thought it might be useful. And she said to give you her . . . er . . . her . . . very best . . . very . . . er . . . love.'

'Has Aunt Eliza been visiting you, then?'

'Yes, last week. Rather inconveniently to say the least. Claims she wrote to warn me. Said I must have overlooked the letter. Never overlooked a letter in my whole life! Harassed me until I agreed I'd come and check up on you, so here I am. It seemed an opportune time to review your progress. Now then, Ermengarde! Where would you like to begin? A little Euclid and then Roman History? Yes? No? Do speak up, my dear! Latin translation? Pray don't bite on your hair like that!'

The meeting had seemed to last for far longer than an hour to Ermengarde, and it was dark before she escaped and fled to the schoolroom. There a gusty sleet-filled wind was causing the fire to smoke so badly that the big girls had gone to their bedrooms, which, although chilly, were at least smoke free. Miss Minchin and Miss Amelia had also been driven away, but Lottie and her friends, who were not allowed to spend their free time anywhere else, were gathered together in a disconsolate huddle, listening as Sara had read a French fairy tale. The little ones were dopey and fretful, uncomfortable with too many clothes and runny noses, but Sara seemed strangely serene.

'*The old fairy,*' Ermengarde heard, '*who wished to make*

him very happy, at last hit upon a plan . . . Ermengarde!'

'Hullo, Sara,' said Ermengarde. 'I have missed you so much! Can I talk to you?'

'The little ones are going upstairs in a minute,' said Sara. 'I must finish their story. They want to know what happened to Prince Hyacinth and the Dear Little Princess, isn't that right, Lottie?'

'They'll get married,' said Lottie, yawning and rubbing her eyes. 'Same as they always do.'

'Don't you want to hear how they managed it, though?'

'*I* would like to hear,' said Ermengarde, trying to be helpful.

'It will be by magic,' said Lottie, while another small girl added, 'I don't think that's fair. I think magic shouldn't be allowed!'

'It's cheating,' agreed Lottie. 'That's what I think. And it's too easy and it's not real life.'

'Oh, Lottie,' said Sara quite crossly. 'How do you know that it isn't real life! And of course it is not cheating! Nor easy! In fact it is very difficult and risky and you never know when it will work. And even then . . . Ermengarde! Are you still here?'

'Yes. Yes I am.'

'Even then, what?' enquired Lottie.

'Even then, it might just melt away. Now. If you little ones don't want to hear the end of the story you had better all collect your things to go upstairs. It must be bedtime now, anyway.'

'Sara, listen,' said Ermengarde urgently, as Lottie and her friends groaned and scuffled and began to scrabble themselves together. 'Miss Minchin is going out this evening! I heard her telling Miss Amelia. She hardly ever goes out, you know, and I do want to talk to you! I have been so worried about you and Becky. So I thought tonight I would come up . . .'

'No!' exclaimed Sara fiercely, and her face was quite white. 'No . . . No, Ermengarde! You mustn't come up again! Anyway, I have to help Miss Amelia tonight. Miss Minchin said. There is a letter to be copied to all the parents and a great deal of mending . . .'

She sounds pleased, thought Ermengarde, very hurt. Pleased that I can't come to see her.

'I shall be in the parlour with her all evening. She said I might work in there because it is so smoky in here . . .'

'Poor Sara!'

'No. No I am not poor Sara. It is not so bad. It is not as bad as you think.'

Sara was already moving towards the schoolroom door, almost as if she wanted to get away. Ermengarde noticed again how thin she had become, and the shabbiness of her worn old shoes. Her feeling of hurt melted away. Sara is cold and tired, she thought, and she doesn't want me to know. A memory came back to her from long ago, when they were both very little.

'You have to bear things,' Sara had said.

She is bearing things now, thought Ermengarde. She is being brave. I should be brave too, to help her.

Ermengarde thought of something cheerful to say.

'It will be nice and warm in the parlour for you. I was there with my papa only a few minutes ago. The fire is not smoky at all.'

Sara nodded.

'I wish you had had the things in the hamper, Sara,' said Ermengarde, all in a rush. 'I don't suppose I shall have another one for a long time now.'

'It doesn't matter,' said Sara. 'Don't worry about it any more. You tried to share. It . . . it made me very happy that you tried to share.'

She hurried away then, but before she left she smiled at Ermengarde, and Ermengarde found herself smiling back. Afterwards she went up to her room quite cheerfully. It was much colder there than downstairs, but she had her red shawl for cosiness, and also the new blue tartan rug that her Aunt Eliza had sent by her father that afternoon.

'Oh,' exclaimed Ermengarde, suddenly seeming to see it for the first time. 'I know what I can do for Sara! There are all sorts things in here that she might have! Why didn't I think of it before?'

The blue tartan rug was the first thing she collected. Then a tin of blackcurrant sweets bought for her sore throat. A new candle. A long-hoarded cake of flower-scented soap. Six ginger biscuits in a pink striped bag. Two apples (one for Becky, thought Ermengarde, beginning to glow) and a little muslin sachet filled with lavender, rose petals and orris root. (For a treat, thought Ermengarde happily.)

Then there was a long wait until the little ones on the floor above settled down to sleep.

At last, very quietly, Ermengarde picked up her bundle of surprises and tiptoed out of the door.

She hesitated at the attic stairs. The attic without Sara was a very eerie place. It was so bare and grey and remote from the rest of the house, the shadows seemed darker there, and the cold, colder. Also, as Becky had once remarked, there were ghosts and spiders and rats 'in waiting'. Sara had laughed at the idea of ghosts, but she had to admit that the spiders and rats were real enough. There was one particular large brown rat that she had named Melchisedec and tamed until he was quite friendly.

Far too friendly, Ermengarde privately thought; she could hear him quite clearly as she stood at the foot of the stairs. He was fat, and he rustled and he ran very quickly.

'Bother Melchisedec!' Ermengarde told herself firmly, shifted her bundle under her arm, climbed the attic stairs, and pushed open the door.

5

In the Attic

IT WAS LIKE WALKING INTO A PICTURE.
A picture in a storybook, a book of fairy tales.

This is what Ermengarde saw:

In the grate there was a glowing, blazing fire; on the hob was a little brass kettle hissing and boiling; spread upon the floor was a thick, warm, crimson rug; before the fire was a folding chair, unfolded, and with cushions on it; by the fire a small folding table, unfolded, covered in a white cloth, and upon it spread small covered dishes, a cup, a saucer, a teapot; on the bed were new warm coverings and a satin-covered down quilt; at the foot a curious wadded silk robe, a pair of quilted slippers, and some books.

The little room was flooded with a warm light from

a bright lamp with a rose-coloured shade that shone on a table.

Ermengarde held the door handle very tightly and began to tremble and she stared and stared.

'Well!' said a voice behind her. *'Well!'*

And it was Lavinia.

Ermengarde pushed blindly past her and ran, scattering biscuits, down the stairs, across the little ones' landing, down the next flight of stairs, and into her own room where she tumbled in a tearless heap on to her own cold little bed.

Sara hadn't told her.

Ermengarde gave a sob and rubbed her eyes and discovered that Lavinia was in the room.

'Here,' said Lavinia, and thrust a handful of biscuits into Ermengarde's bundle and plumped down on the bed beside her.

'You didn't know,' Lavinia said.

It was a statement, not a question, and there was an expression on Lavinia's face that Ermengrade had never seen before.

'What are you going to do now?' Lavinia asked.

'Do?' repeated Ermengarde, sitting up. 'I'm not going

to do anything. And neither are you!'

'Oh?'

'If you tell,' Ermengarde whispered fiercely, 'if you tell, like you did before about Aunt Eliza's hamper, I will, I will . . .'

'What?' asked Lavinia.

'Cut off your hair!'

Lavinia's hands involuntarily flew to her curls.

'*Cut off my hair?*'

'If you tell I will. And you needn't say I couldn't because I could. With my sewing scissors. While you are asleep . . .'

But Lavinia was hardly listening; her eyes had strayed to the contents of Ermengrade's bundle, now tumbled all over the bed. 'You didn't know,' she said again. 'You couldn't have. Why would you have taken those things if you did?'

'You mind your own business!'

'I thought you and Sara were supposed to be friends!'

'What do you know about anything?' demanded Ermengarde stormily. 'Go away, Lavinia Herbert, and remember what I warned you would happen if you told!'

'As if you would dare!' said Lavinia.

6

Diamonds Change Everything

THE FOLLOWING WEEK OF THAT WINTER
term was the one that Jessica remembered most wistfully
in the dull January that came afterwards.

'Cataclysmic event upon cataclysmic event,' remarked
Lavinia.

'*What* upon *what*?' enquired Jessie.

'A cataclysmic event, Jessica,' said Lavinia, 'is one
which causes enormous and astonishing and destructive
upheaval, such as the eruption of Mount Vesuvius.
Ermengarde knows what I'm talking about, don't
you, Ermie?'

She glared at Ermengarde through half-closed eyes,

and Ermengarde glared back. Lavinia had awoken that day to find a newly shorn curl of blonde hair laid neatly on her bedside table. No word had been spoken on the subject by either of them, but there was a new feeling between them. A sort of understanding.

The latest cataclysmic event had been the acquisition by Sara of a truly sumptuous new frock.

'Yes, and that's not all!' said Jessica eagerly. 'It isn't just one frock! I saw her unpacking in the hall. There were parcels and parcels of lovely clothes!'

'Lovely?' asked Lavinia.

'You know they are, Lavvie.'

It was true, they were lovely, and most unsuitable for anyone who spent as much time working with the scullery maid as Sara was required to do. Miss Minchin evidently realised this herself. Very soon after the parcels had been unpacked the schoolroom door opened and the pupils of the Select Seminary gave a concerted gasp.

It was as if time had turned back two years.

It was Princess Sara.

She was taller, and her face was no longer childish and

eager, but except for those things she looked exactly like the Sara of the past. And, just as had happened when she first pushed open the schoolroom door, six years before, she was given Lavinia's place, the seat of honour closest to Miss Minchin. Once again, Lavinia was demoted to second-best pupil, and she did not enjoy it any more now than she had done the first time it happened.

'Sara did say she'd rather not have that seat,' mentioned Jessie to Ermengarde later that morning. 'But Miss Minchin said she must. I do think it is rather hard on Lavvie. And *where* did it all come from, Ermengarde?'

That was the question that everyone whispered as soon as Sara left the room.

'Ask her, Ermie!' begged Jessica.

'No.'

'You then, Lavinia!'

'Are you implying that I have the slightest interest?' asked Lavinia, scornfully.

'Lottie,' implored Jessica. 'Go and catch Sara when she comes back and ask her what has been happening!'

Lottie was more than happy to help, and she did it very excitedly, jumping up and down before Sara and gripping her hands.

'I call it The Magic,' said Sara, and her dark eyelashes dropped to veil her enormous green eyes, and she detached herself very gently from Lottie, and slipped from the room.

Two days later she had vanished completely.

Then, instead of whispers, a wild flocking chattering had echoed and speculated all through the house. It flew through the bedrooms and landings and stairs, and in the schoolroom the noise was loudest of all.

Becky was seized for questioning.

'Miss Sara,' said Becky, 'has took next door's monkey back. It escaped in the night. With her umbrella that came new the other day.'

'The monkey *escaped* with the umbrella?' asked Jessie.

'No, no,' said Becky. 'Miss Sara, *with* her umbrella because it has been coming down in stair rods since before six this morning, *took* the monkey round to the people next door because they are very sensitive.'

'The people next door are very sensitive?' asked Gertrude.

'Not the people,' said Becky. 'Them little monkeys! Them little monkeys are very sensitive, Miss Sara said. I don't know nothing about the next door *people*. She seen them before in India.'

'What? The people from next door?'

'*The monkeys*, Miss Jessica! Miss Sara knows all about them sort of monkeys, what they needs and how to care for them, and that's why she's took it. It belongs to that Indian gentleman next door but he's not fit. I better go else Miss Minchin will say I'm gossiping with the young ladies.'

'Is it anything to do with her new clothes?'

'I couldn't say, I'm sure,' said Becky primly, and left the room.

'I'm sure it is,' said Jessie, when she was gone, 'but it's all so puzzling. I could understand if the clothes had come *after* the monkey, as a sort of thank you, although even then it would seem a bit much. Becky said it was only a little monkey . . . And why should that put Miss Minchin into such a terrible temper? I heard her scolding, and I'm sure I heard Sara's name.'

'You are making it all too complicated,' announced Lavinia airily. 'It is perfectly plain to me. Princess Sara has taken a monkey back to its owner who lives next door. She has not come back and Miss Minchin is angry because the potatoes need peeling or something like that. Possibly Sara will never come back. They may be able to give her a job as full-time monkey keeper. Her clothes are just right, and I'm sure she'd be good at it, she has had so much practice with Lottie.'

This suggestion had caused a great deal of laughter; they were still laughing when the schoolroom door opened and Ermengarde came in.

Ermengarde was staring at a letter. A letter that she was holding very tightly in both hands as if it might suddenly take off and fly. Her face was stunned.

'What is the matter, Ermie?' asked Jessica. 'Not another message from your papa asking when you are going to start studying Greek?'

'I . . . I . . .' began Ermengarde, stammering a little with amazement. 'I have just had this letter from Sara!'

It was the final cataclysm of that cataclysmic week.

That was how the school learned that Sara (previous princess, present-time servant, potential monkey keeper) was, most astonishingly of all, the long-sought heiress of an enormous fortune. Owner, in fact, of several diamond mines, all of them, if Ermengarde was to be believed, stuffed and sparkling with millions and millions and millions of diamonds. And as well as the diamonds, it seemed, she had a new guardian in the shape of the very rich, also diamond-laden, Indian gentleman next door.

'How very jolly for her,' said Lavinia, some time later, when the initial uproar had died down. 'Especially as her new guardian looks so extremely ill. I suppose it won't be long before Sara inherits his diamonds too.'

'What a horrible thing to say!' exclaimed Ermengarde.

'Not horrible at all,' said Lavinia. 'Simply facing facts. People the colour he is usually have liver disease. He probably caught it in India. It is a very germy country, I believe. Will Sara be going to live there?'

'Why ever should she?'

'She has to live somewhere,' said Lavinia reasonably. 'And what would be the point of staying next door (except to annoy poor Miss Minchin of course). India is the obvious place. She may want to go and watch her diamonds being shovelled into the sacks, I suppose. Anyway, she obviously won't be coming back here . . .

Ermengarde, would you rather we told you when your mouth had fallen open, or do you prefer to just leave it to gape?'

7

Changes

THE NEXT CHAPTER OF THE STORY TOOK place over the Christmas holidays.

As always, Ermengarde spent Christmas with her father.

Ermengarde's father's idea of Christmas consisted of a succession of large meals in intelligent company. Usually Ermengarde escaped this torment, but this year, being considered by her father to be nearly grown up ('I'm not thirteen until next month!' she protested in vain) she did not. Ermengarde had a more or less horrible Christmas. Her Aunt Eliza was away visiting friends and there were no parties or outings.

'Fancy not doing *anything*!' Jessica had exclaimed

when they got back to school.

'I didn't say I didn't do *anything*,' Ermengarde replied.

They had returned that term to find that changes had already taken place at the house next door. It was rented to new people. Sara was gone.

'I knew she would,' said Lavinia. 'I told you so, Ermengarde!'

'I knew,' said Ermengarde with dignity. 'I visited her in the holidays. Three times . . . (So there, Jessica! I didn't not do anything!) She told me she would be going away. They are staying at the seaside because the Indian gentleman who she calls Uncle Tom is not very well. I met him when I visited, and the monkey and Sara's huge new dog.'

'Has Sara a huge new dog?' asked Lottie enviously.

'Yes, the Indian gentleman bought him for a surprise for her just before they went away. He is called Boris and he is a boar hound.'

'Fascinating to think of Princess Sara boar hunting,' said Lavinia.

'Did you see any diamonds, Ermie, while you were there?' enquired Jessica hopefully. 'Has Sara any of her own yet?'

'Of course she has, silly!' said Lavinia, who was in a remarkably bad temper this term, perhaps because she had been one of the unfortunates left in the school over Christmas. 'Diamonds are as common as sugar lumps to Sara these days.'

'I don't think I saw any diamonds,' said Ermengarde, 'but Boris does have a gold and silver collar with an inscription on it that says, "*I am Boris. I serve the Princess Sara.*"'

'How truly vulgar,' remarked Lavinia, preparing to leave the room. 'Come with me, Jessie, and I will show you my new mink dressing gown. It has emerald buttons and pearl-encrusted pockets. I am planning to wear it to church on Sunday to show how rich I am.'

Jessie giggled, and got up to follow, but lingered at the door for one last question.

'Are you and Sara still best friends, Ermie?'

'We have always been best friends,' said Ermengarde, staunchly. 'Why should anything change?'

All the same, the friendship had changed, and Ermengarde knew it. For one thing, she and Sara had stopped sharing.

Ever since they were little girls Sara and Ermengarde had shared. Books and stories and dolls and treats. They had shared the warmth of the schoolroom fire, and later the cold of the attic. They shared unhappiness:

'My papa says I am a fool,' said Ermengarde (it was almost the first thing she told Sara about herself), 'like my Aunt Eliza.'

'Well, he is wrong,' stated Sara flatly.

And they had shared worries:

'Ermie,' said Sara, sometime after she had moved up into the attic, 'is my voice . . . you know, the way I speak . . . is it the same as it always was?'

'I think so,' said Ermengarde, starting in surprise at this question.

'It hasn't become a little like . . . like Becky's? Or Cook's?'

'*Cook's?*' asked Ermengarde. '*Cook's?*' And then she had laughed so much that she had almost fallen off Sara's little attic bed.

And they had shared just plain talking:

'There was a princess,' related Sara, 'who kissed a frog, and he turned straight away into a handsome prince and he fell in love with her.'

'He must have been an odd sort of prince,' said Ermengarde. 'To fall in love with someone who kisses frogs.'

When Ermengarde had returned to school after the Christmas holiday she found that she missed more than anything the simple pleasure of having someone to whom she could talk.

There had been plenty of talk over the holidays. Dozens of things had been discussed: Miss Minchin's and Boris and diamonds and books and dresses and princesses and what good friends they would always be, and how pleased Ermengarde was that the diamond mines belonging to Sara were so full of diamonds, and how sure Sara was that Ermengarde would one day make friends with her papa . . .

'Sara, I am not a bit the sort of person my papa likes for a friend,' said Ermengarde. 'You should see his friends and then you would understand. They are all so clever and whiskery and they smoke pipes and make jokes in Greek and Latin. I should *never* dare to try to be friends with my papa!'

'That's not very brave,' said Sara, laughing.

'No,' agreed Ermengarde. 'I know it isn't. I'm not brave. You know that though, Sara.'

Then, although neither of them quite knew why, there was an uncomfortable silence.

It was not the first uncomfortable silence of the holidays, there had been several. Often the conversations had suddenly stopped and Ermengarde had found Sara glancing away from her eyes.

There are so many things we don't say, thought Ermengarde.

They didn't talk about Becky, not after Ermengarde had innocently asked, 'What will she do?' thinking that Becky might be destined for a new future too, school, perhaps, and later a small share in the diamonds.

'*Do?*' asked Sara.

Nor did they talk about Sara's sudden new guardian, Uncle Tom, who had taken such ages to find her. 'My papa says he should have asked at your papa's bank,' said Ermengarde. 'They would have known where you were in a moment, my papa says, because of paying Miss Minchin's bills for so long. Didn't your Uncle Tom think of that, Sara?'

'It is kind of your papa to be interested,' said Sara, 'but

he can't possibly understand.'

'No, I suppose not,' agreed Ermengarde humbly, and tried to change the conversation to a more cheerful subject. 'Do you still have your doll, Emily, Sara? If she was left behind I could creep up to the attic and find her for you, when I go back next term.'

'I have her upstairs in my room,' said Sara. 'Thank you, Ermie, but the day after I came away Miss Amelia packed all my things in my old trunk and sent it here.'

'*All* your things?' asked Ermengarde, remembering the books and cushions and bowls of flowers, the rosy lamp and silky cushions, the hundred treasures of the little attic room.

'Yes.'

'In that one little trunk?'

'Yes,' said Sara, and her eyes slid away from Ermengarde's, so Ermengarde stopped asking questions.

All that holiday Sara never once mentioned the transformation that had taken place in the attic.

Why not? wondered Ermengarde, more hurt and uncomprehending with each day of silence. Sara was safe now. She need not fear Miss Minchin or anyone else any more. So why did she never even *begin* to say, 'Ermie, I wish you had seen . . .' Then I could say, 'Yes! I did! And your secret was quite safe! I tiptoed away and I didn't tell, and neither did Lavinia. Do you know how I stopped her? I crept into her room and cut off a curl of her hair! With my sewing scissors! I have been longing to tell you. I was only waiting for you to begin!'

'Ermie, I wish . . .' began Sara on their last afternoon together, and for a moment Ermengarde thought that the secret was going to be shared at last, but Sara went on, 'Ermie, will you do something for me next term?'

'Yes of course, if I can,' said Ermengarde, rather flatly.

'I *think* you can,' said Sara. 'Anyway you could try. It's Lottie.'

'Lottie?'

'I always tried to stop her getting into trouble. And to take care of her a little. I won't be able to do that any more. I thought you might, Ermie.'

'Oh, *Sara*!' exclaimed Ermengarde, horrified. 'Oh, I can't! Think how the girls would laugh at me! Lavinia and Jessie and the rest! And Lottie is so naughty . . .'

'There is no one else to ask,' said Sara.

It is over, thought Ermengarde. Being best friends is over. Sharing is over. Now it is just looking after Lottie because there is no one else to ask.

However, long ago, when she was only seven years old, Ermengarde had said to Sara: 'I wish we could be best friends.'

Fours years later, when everything had changed, she had climbed to the attic and saved that friendship.

If it's over, it's over, thought Ermengarde solidly, and that's that.

Still, for the sake of the friendship that once had been, she said, 'I don't know if I can look after Lottie. I don't know if she will let me. But . . .' Ermengarde gulped. 'I'll try.'

8

Alice

AFTER CHRISTMAS AT MISS MINCHIN'S
there was a different feeling in the air. It was not just that
Sara had gone. Or that Becky had been replaced by a
new maid called Alice. Nor even that half a dozen girls
had left for home at Christmas and simply not returned,
although that certainly led to speculation.

'I expect they told,' said Jessica. 'You know, about the
way Miss Minchin treated Sara after she thought there
was no money. And how Sara disappeared to the Indian
gentleman's house.'

'She didn't *disappear*,' put in Ermengarde. 'She
just *went*.'

'And those days at the end of term when Miss Minchin

shut herself up and wouldn't speak to anyone,' continued Jessica, ignoring Ermengarde's objection, 'and then the doctor and that other man breaking down her bedroom door . . .'

'They did not break down the door!' snapped Lavinia. 'They unscrewed the lock. It was jammed. Don't exaggerate, Jessie! Did you tell your parents all that rubbish?'

'It isn't rubbish and yes I did and they were very shocked and they said that I need not come back if I liked.'

'Then why on earth did you?' demanded Lavinia.

'Well!' exclaimed Jessica. 'Well! And what would you have done, Lavinia, if I hadn't?'

Amongst all the differences and changes at the Select Seminary, the greatest of all was in Miss Minchin herself.

'She makes Miss Amelia do nearly all of the teaching,' said Lottie. 'Most mornings she just starts the big girls off and goes away. And she doesn't look the same. Her hair used to look like it was painted on with treacle, but it doesn't any more. You can see grey bits. And her skin is so pale and her eyes are so pink . . .'

'Hush, Lottie!' Ermengarde suddenly remembered that she was supposed to be looking after Lottie and glanced nervously over her shoulder.

'And she has a new smell!'

'Lottie!' said Ermengarde. 'You should never ever talk about how anybody smells!'

'But it is an *interesting* smell!' said Lottie. 'Not nasty! I almost like it in a way! Ermie, do you know what I think? I think Miss Minchin is missing Sara!'

'She didn't even *like* Sara,' said Ermengarde.

'You can miss things you don't like,' said Lottie. 'I didn't like my hair, but I missed it when I chopped it off. I couldn't get used to it being gone. I think Miss Minchin can't get used to Sara being gone. At the very end of last term, while Sara was staying next door, and Miss Minchin was shut up in her room, she used to watch out of the windows for her. I noticed when we went for walks.'

'Goodness, Lottie!'

'And I think she's still watching for her. In case she comes back.'

Lottie the school baby, Ermengarde realised, was a

baby no more. She no longer lay on the floor and howled. She chopped off her curls and noticed things.

'She is a holy terror,' said Alice, the new maid.

Alice was the last of the changes at Miss Minchin's. It was Alice who said, 'That attic is a very nasty place.'

The attic had been Alice's first battleground at the Select Seminary. On the afternoon of her arrival she was taken there with her bag, Cook leading the way, Miss Amelia panting behind.

'No thank you very much!' Alice said after one scornful sniff, and she had hefted her bag up to her chest and added that she had a good home in Epping and would now be getting herself back.

'I shall hand in my notice this very moment,' remarked Cook at this point, 'if I have to put up with one more day in that kitchen with no proper help.'

At this threat Miss Amelia became very alarmed. She was the improper help to which Cook referred. Since Becky left she had spent a good many afternoons buttering bread and boiling cocoa and she had not enjoyed the experience. If Cook left, things would become far more unpleasant. Horrible vision of joints and cabbages and porridge and puddings all requiring

her unaccomplished attention filled her mind.

'Come downstairs at once, Alice dear,' she said, quite faint at the prospect, 'and we will all have a cup of tea and talk about it calmly.'

Alice drank her tea with her bag on her lap and a very determined expression on her face which did not disappear until a snug little cupboard of a room had been discovered beside the kitchen, next door to Cook and with a view of the basement steps.

'That's more like it,' said Alice, and put down her bag at last.

And so the attic rooms were left empty and undisturbed. Cobwebs blurred the corners and the dust of London sifted in through the tiles and joined the patches of mildew already blooming on the hard little beds where Sara and Becky once had slept. A fall of soot from Sara's chimney fanned out like a shadow in one corner. Every smell in the house, from the cabbages in the kitchen to the interesting new aroma that Lottie had noticed on Miss Minchin, drifted and rose and accumulated there.

* * *

'A very nasty place,' said Alice.

'It was always considered perfectly suitable in the past,' said Miss Amelia privately to Cook.

'Times have changed,' said Cook, meaningfully, 'since that young madam . . .'

'Miss Sara,' murmured Miss Amelia.

'. . . Miss Diamond Mines! Took herself off, didn't she! And now she's away to the seaside I hear, for air, along with that Indian gentlemen. Although why they need air more than the rest of us I'm sure I can't say! And that lazy young monkey, Becky, gone with them without a by your leave, after all I've done for her! And what do we get instead? This Alice-from-Epping who won't be called a scullery maid . . .' ('I don't care to be called one of them,' Alice had stated. 'And I won't!')

'. . . and doesn't like attics! Not that I blame her there, mind you! Because if you ask me, there's something very fishy about that attic, and always was. Others have said the same.'

'Have they?'

'Noises, so I hear . . . and the damp is undeniable and Alice claims it smells of rats! "Are you that familiar with the smell of rats, then, my lady?" I wanted to ask, but I couldn't because she would pack that bag of hers and be off, like as not . . . Where *is* the girl? She might be back in Epping for all the use she is half the time! Can I ask you to make a start on chopping some suet, Miss Amelia? That slab over there? . . . Yes, noises, the maids say. Whispers!'

'Whispers?' asked Alice, sauntering into the kitchen as if she owned the place. 'What whispers?'

'Alice, here you are at last!' exclaimed Miss Amelia, handing over the suet knife, and laughing aloud in relief. 'Whispers! Really! What nonsense!'

'Probably nothing more than the sparrows on the roof,' said Miss Amelia.

9

Ermengarde's Birthday
(Part Two)

IN THE SCHOOLROOM, LATE ON THE afternoon of Ermengarde's thirteenth birthday, the sparrow voices were suddenly excited.

The boy from next door has just walked past! He stood under the street lamp and looked right in at us! He has hair like flames. He is studying with his uncle. He is very ill. He is very clever.

'He winked at me,' said Jessica, smirking.

'Oh, Jessie, fancy being pleased!'

'One day,' said Jessie, 'we will be eighteen and we will be Presented. And then we will be Out. There will be boys then, Lavvie! And balls and parties and dancing and proposals. And I will meet someone wonderful, with black hair and black eyes and a house in the country quite near our house at home, and lots of money. And we will have six children, all dear little girls. I've chosen their names already . . .'

'You'd better marry him first,' said Lavinia, sourly.

'Of course I will! Probably in St Paul's and I will have a white lace dress with a veil and a white foamy train and I will carry white roses and pink rosebuds tied with pink floating ribbons and the bridesmaids will wear pink too . . .'

'Pink is the colour of ham,' remarked Lottie. 'Couldn't they wear orange? Or green or yellow?'

'Don't be silly, Lottie!'

'It is you who are silly!' Lavinia, who usually ignored conversations of this sort, suddenly seemed to be furious. 'Balls and parties and proposals and roses!' she repeated scornfully. 'Six children, all girls! What do you suppose you will do with six children, all girls? Send them to Miss Minchin's?'

'Goodness, Lavvie, what a temper you are in!' said Jessie, admiring her hair in the window.

'Don't you see what all that is? The balls and parties

and the dear little girls?'

'What?'

'It's a trap!' said Lavinia.

'A trap?' asked Jessie, turning round from the window in surprise.

'That's right. Oh, for goodness' sake close the curtains! No wonder people look in! A trap for stupid girls! Our grandmothers fell into it, and our mothers, and you will be next, Jessie! And you will never learn anything or go anywhere or do anything that matters! And your six stupid girls will be just the same, admiring their hair and planning pink dresses and staring out of the window at horrible boys . . .'

'Lavvie, don't cry!'

'I'm not! How dare you say that!'

'You're just jealous,' said Gertrude, 'because he winked at Jessie!'

Lavinia got up and walked out of the schoolroom, banging the door.

'Good riddance!' said Gertrude.

'Everyone is so bad-tempered!' complained Jessie. 'Oh, Ermengarde, have you *another* cold? Must you always sniff?'

'I suppose I can sniff if I want to,' said Ermengarde. 'Since it is January and it has rained all day and everyone is so hateful and I have chilblains and it is my birthday and here I am at Miss Minchin's just like last year and the year before and the year before and the year before . . . Lavinia is right, it *is* a trap . . . Oh!'

Ermengarde jumped as the door opened, but it was only Alice, come to check the fire.

Alice immediately set about organising everyone.

'Put a little coal on the fire, Miss Jessie, do!' she exclaimed as she came in. 'Fancy big girls like you and can't make up a fire! Sweep up those cinders while you're down there, my dear, and some of you straighten those rugs! Miss Ermengarde, use a handkerchief, please! If there's one thing I cannot abide, it is sniffing!'

Alice was, as Cook described her, plain as a pudding and built like a gate. She was the eldest of a large family, and much more accustomed to ordering people about than taking orders herself. But she was a worker. While she talked she straightened the curtains, lined up the chairs, blew on the mantelpiece and polished it with her apron, and hauled Lottie, who had been sprawled on the hearth rug, briskly to her feet.

'Look at you, all bits from the floor!' she scolded. 'Stand up while I get at you!'

Lottie obeyed. They all did more or less as Alice told them. They were becoming accustomed to her way of treating them exactly as she treated the children at home. But all the same, she was the most unusual maid they had ever known.

'You're not a bit like Becky, Alice,' observed Jessie, watching as Alice hit dust off Lottie with hands like red spades.

'And what was she like, pray?' demanded Alice. 'A fashion plate? A Superior Nursemaid? A slave which enjoyed running around after you lazy misses?'

'She was very humble . . .' said Jessie.

'Oh, humble,' said Alice, lifting Lottie's curls to peer underneath. 'You need a good scrub on this neck, young lady, and behind your ears! Let me see your hands!'

'. . . She was very thin, too, and small . . .'

'All us Rileys are big-boned,' said Alice. 'That's jam on your sleeve, my girl, and licking it doesn't make it any better!'

'. . . and she slept in the attic.'

'You'd be pretty if you were clean!' said Alice, kissing

the top of Lottie's head. 'Slept in the attic indeed! They showed it to me. There's rats in there or I'm a Dutchman. And cold as a tomb and about as cheerful. I don't know how anyone could stay in such a place and keep their self-respect . . . Now what did I say to make Miss Ermengarde go slamming out like that?'

'Everyone is slamming out today,' said Jessie. 'It was Lavinia earlier. I suppose Ermie was thinking about Sara, her friend. She used to sleep in the attic. Hasn't anyone told you about Sara?'

'Her with the diamonds? Was she Miss Ermengarde's friend?'

'Yes, and poor Ermie misses her terribly.'

Alice asked no more questions, but later in the evening she went upstairs and tapped on Ermengarde's door and announced that she had come to brush her hair.

'Since it is your birthday,' she said cheerfully. 'Sit up properly now, and let me unknot that bit of ribbon. What colour was it when it was new?'

'Blue,' said Ermengarde, sitting up as she was told because it was easier than arguing. 'It still is blue!'

'Not where you've chewed it, it's not,' said Alice, beginning to brush. 'Now don't tell me I'm pulling because I happen to know I am not. This is a job I'm very good at. Which I should be, having three little sisters, not to mention Clara who has hair down to her waist.'

'Who is Clara?'

'She's my friend in Epping. She's the one I tell things to, if you understand what I mean. Clara Pie, her name is, and it always looks very funny to me written down on an envelope.'

'I suppose it does.'

'I write to her every Sunday, you see, and Clara, she writes back every Wednesday.'

'I write to my papa on Sundays,' said Ermengarde, rather dolefully. 'It's terribly difficult. I can never think of anything to say when I have to speak to him, and I can never think of anything when I write to him either.'

'Sometimes we put things in for each other,' continued Alice, ignoring this gloomy interruption. 'Like last week Clara put in an early snowdrop for me, pressed on a piece of card.'

'It would be no good sending my papa snowdrops,' said Ermengarde, even more dismally.

'Bother your papa!' said Alice. 'I wasn't thinking of him!'

'I was only explaining,' explained Ermengarde, 'that he would think it was ridiculous. He would say it was exactly the sort of thing my Aunt Eliza might do.'

'Bother your Aunt Eliza too!' said Alice. 'I wasn't thinking of her either!'

'My papa says my Aunt Eliza is the silliest woman in the world,' remarked Ermengarde.

Alice refused to take any more interest in Ermengarde's Aunt Eliza than she had in the probable effect of sending snowdrops to Mr St John. She lost her temper, in the sudden way she had of doing that, snapped, 'Really! I don't known why I bother!' and re-plaited Ermengarde's hair so tightly that the resulting pigtail was as solid as if it had been carved out of wood.

Ermengarde took herself disconsolately off to bed, but hours and hours later, deep in the middle of the night, an idea drifted through her dreams and into her mind. She didn't know it was Alice's; she thought it was all her own.

I will write to Sara! thought Ermengarde. I could do that! It would be better than nothing, anyway.

Looking After Lottie

IT WAS ONE THING FOR ERMENGARDE TO think of writing to Sara, but it was quite another to make up her mind to actually do it. On Sunday she wrote her compulsory weekly letter to her father and was so desperate for something to fill the page that she copied out the French poem Miss Amelia had ordered they all learn. It got the poem into her head a little more, but it gave her such a stomach ache doing it that all she could manage to Sara was a picture postcard saying, *Thank you for the book.*

Lottie, who was still at the enviable age of too-little-to-write-without-Miss-Amelia's-help ('although I'm sure I had to write home without help when I was eight,' grumbled Ermengarde), wandered around the schoolroom annoying people while the letter writting torment was in progress.

'Bump my elbow one more time and I'll slay you,' Lavinia told her. 'Go away ... further than that ... further than that ... Now, don't come any closer!'

'But then I will just be walking round the edges of the room!' objected Lottie, picking up a piece of paper from the floor. 'Can I have this to make a boat out of? Oh, the ink's still all wet! Look at my hands! Let me past to the curtains quick!'

'Lottie!' exploded Jessie as Lottie rubbed her inky hands on the schoolroom curtains (which Miss Minchin had sensibly chosen in a dismal but useful shade of blueish-grey). 'Have you picked up my first page to Mamma? Is that it? Oh you are a nuisance! I shall have to write it out all over again!'

'I could help you,' offered Lottie.

'I thought you were supposed to be too little to write!'

'I can write,' said Lottie. 'I just like to let Miss Amelia do it. She is faster than me. *I* write "Dearest Papa, I hope you are well," and then *she* does the middle bit about how good I am and clever and things, and then *I* write "with love Lottie may I have some rabbits when I come home?" and it's done in no time. What is that picture you are sending to Sara, Ermie?'

'The Tower.'

'What tower?'

'The Tower of London. I thought it was pretty.'

'*You thought the Tower of London was pretty?*' repeated Lavinia. 'It's a prison, for goodness sake!'

'Is it?' asked Lottie. 'Oh, I've got a lovely idea! Let me take it a minute! I'll be very careful! There!'

Lavinia laughed, Lottie smirked, Jessica and several others sniggered, and Ermengarde put her head down on her table and wailed. Every bit of post that left the school was first checked by Miss Minchin or Miss Amelia. This card was now doomed.

MISS MINCHINS SLECKT SEMINRY

read a row of black capitals across the top and a bedraggled-looking raven glowering in the foreground was labelled with an arrow

MISS MINCHIN

'I shall have to throw it away,' lamented Ermengarde. 'And I'd even put the stamp on! Lottie, you are a nuisance!'

'Sara will laugh,' said Lottie.

'Miss Minchin won't.'

'Oh!' exclaimed Lottie. 'Oh, Ermie, I'm sorry! I didn't think. I forgot she would see it. Never mind, give it to me! I know what to do!'

She grabbed the card a second time, and slid out of the room. Ten minutes later she was back, very cold and damp but triumphant.

'Posted!' she whispered.

'Lottie! How?'

'In the box by the wall on the way to church.'

'But how did you get out?'

'It's easy to get out,' said Lottie, ''specially now Miss Minchin is in her room so much. And with Alice coming from Epping. That helps.'

'What *are* you talking about?'

'There is so much fresh air in Epping, you see,' said Lottie, and would say no more, despite all their questions.

'Don't you trust us?' asked Jessica.

'Of course I don't,' said Lottie, sounding very surprised at such a silly idea.

'Have you done it before?'

Lottie smiled.

'What if something awful happens to you while you're out there?'

'What if something awful happens to me while I'm in here?' asked Lottie.

'Oh!' growled Jessica impatiently. 'You just shouldn't do it! You're much too little. Tell her she shouldn't, Ermengarde!'

'Me?' asked Ermengarde. 'Oh well, no, you shouldn't really, Lottie. Not without someone to look after you.'

'I can look after myself,' said Lottie, swinging gently on the curtains. 'Who wants to play going round and round the room without touching the floor?'

'Not on a Sunday,' said Ermengarde, but Lottie played it anyway, all by herself, until the inevitable painful inky disaster caused her to be led away roaring by Miss Amelia.

'I believe your behaviour is becoming worse and worse!' scolded Miss Amelia. 'Sara Crewe was the only one who could manage you! Lavinia, ring for Alice, please! Ermengarde, you have stood in spilled ink! You are leaving inky footmarks! No, don't wipe your shoe on your stocking! Take it off!'

Ermengarde took her shoe off and put her stockinged foot down in a puddle of ink and was sent upstairs in disgrace. There, having nothing else to do, she finally began writing to Sara.

Ermengarde wrote:

> *You said, 'Look after Lottie,' Well, that is not easy, Sara. 'She is such a darling,' you said, but she has not been a darling lately. This afternoon she has not been a darling at all, and that is one of the reasons I am up here in the cold while everyone else is downstairs. She has been bad since the holidays, Sara, and because she is the leader of the little ones and they all do as she says, they have been bad too. This term, because there are only eight of them, Miss Minchin and Miss Amelia have put them to sleep together in the big room over our parlour bedrooms. It used to be the nursery, Miss Amelia told them, when she was little. And it still has bars on the windows and I think that is a good thing because Lottie is so naughty I am sure she would climb out if she thought she could.*

Ermengarde paused, and looked down at her letter with astonishment. This was not like writing to her father! Here was a page full already, with no effort at all! It was as easy as breathing, easier than talking!

The bars made Lottie invent a new game for bedtime called Zoo Animals. They are each a different animal every night. They make a terrible noise bouncing into their beds which they call dens and lairs and caves and things. Lottie is the worst. At least the others stop being Zoo Animals to say their prayers but Lottie does not. I know because not long ago she said, 'Come and tuck me in, Ermie. Come and hear my prayers like Sara used to do.' And so I went up and she was hopping around on one leg saying she was a flamingo and her prayer was:

> *Dear God*
> *I think, I would rather be the only*
> *green flamingo in the world. Than pink.*

Nothing happened to her! I am sure if I ever prayed a prayer like that I would be struck down dead.
I said this to Lottie.
'God is used to me,' said Lottie.

Ermengarde reached for another sheet of paper. Words were flying from her pen as if she had no part in the matter.

Of course, after I had tucked Lottie in all the other seven wanted to be tucked in too, and then they said, 'Tell us a story, Ermie! Tell us a story like Sara used to do!' And they

growled and baaed and squeaked and made flamingo noises
until I thought Miss Minchin would hear.

Ermengarde's handwriting was sloping and wispy and
not very straight. Very soon the pages began to look as
if they were scattered with dark feathers.

> *The only story that came into my head was an awful one*
> *you and I read together. It was about a little girl called*
> *Karen who had a pair of red dancing shoes that she thought*
> *about all the time. Even in church instead of saying her*
> *prayers. I expect you remember it better than me, Sara, but*
> *I remembered enough to make it into a story. It quietened*
> *the little ones very quickly. I thought it would. Especially*
> *the bit at the end where Karen goes to the axeman and has*
> *her feet chopped off and the shoes with her feet in go dancing*
> *away.*
>
> *They loved it.*
>
> *Only in the middle of the night I heard a terrible noise*
> *right over my head and it was Lottie shrieking that she*
> *could hear the red shoes dancing. And all the others started*
> *too. I shall have to go up, I thought, but I did not want to.*
> *And then suddenly I heard Miss Minchin's voice louder*
> *than all of the little ones howling together. And then it was*
> *quiet.*

As Ermengarde wrote, her mind became more and more
peaceful. It was like tidying a cupboard, clearing away

the clutter. It was like shedding a heavy cloak. It was like opening a window.

She brought her letter down with her after supper.

'Who are you writing to?' asked Lottie, back in the schoolroom again, cleaned and bandaged and peering over Ermengarde's shoulder.

'Sara. About last night.'

'I *did* hear the red shoes,' said Lottie. 'They came into my dream and danced around my bed. I was so frightened that I was pleased to see Miss Minchin. She was so real and cross and she was smelling very strongly of her nice new smell! She wanted to know where we had heard such a ridiculous tale. Someone started to say Ermengarde but I saved you, Ermie! I said it was a story Sara knew.'

'What did Miss Minchin say then?'

'She said, "I might have guessed", and the bones in her face went red like they do when she is angry and she swished out of the room so quickly her candle blew out. But I expect she knew her way in the dark. Ermie?'

'Hmmm?'

'You should write to Sara about Lavinia and The Boy.'

II

Lavinia and The Boy

Lottie says I should tell you about The Boy. She means the boy who has moved in next door, to the house where the Indian gentleman stayed while he was searching for you. Lottie is fascinated by him, and so is Jessie. I think he is older than any of us, but I have only seen him for a moment as he passed the window, and then I did not really notice anything except his hair. I have been looking around this room, Sara, for something the same colour as his hair so that I could explain it to you. The only thing I can see is the reddy gold bit in the bottom of the fire. But that is too red; it is darker than that. I have never seen a person with hair like dark fire before.

The boy came here last Friday. To us, the Young Ladies' Select Seminary. I wonder if a boy has ever walked through our door before.

Alice the new maid answered the bell. (She says he is as

white as death and has a terrible cough.) Anyway, Alice let him in and brought him to Miss Minchin's parlour. Miss Minchin was in there with Lavinia because she has started giving Lavvie English literature classes all by herself. Lavinia asked her if she would, and she agreed straight away. Lavinia always was her favourite, you know, Sara. Only you were so rich, you see, that you had to have first place. Do you know what I think, too? I think Miss Minchin was always a little bit frightened of you.

Anyway, that does not matter now.

Miss Minchin was reading Henry the Fifth to Lavinia (which is a play by William Shakespeare about Henry V) and she was reading it in a rather loud voice because she had got to a very famous bit where the king shouts a lot. Alice showed the boy in without knocking and Miss Minchin did not notice he was there at first. And then she did and she went all quiet while he introduced himself. (Jessie saw all this through the door hinge crack, because as soon as she heard Alice let the boy in she slipped out to see what was happening.) The boy told his name (which is Tristram) and that he was staying with his uncle who tutors people for university, and that he was being tutored too, because he has missed a lot of school, being ill. And the boy also said they have a cat and that the cat was lost because it had not liked moving house, and so he had called to ask if we had seen it. And if we did would we send it back.

By the time he had said all this, Miss Minchin had got over being caught shouting about battles and she was very stiff and gracious. She said to the boy that perhaps he had not realised that this was not only a private home but also a Young Ladies' Select Seminary. And then, just as she said those words, Jessie had to dodge out of sight because Miss Amelia came panting up from the kitchen with an enormous pudding on a plate and she rushed straight into Miss Minchin's room with it saying, 'Would you look at this pudding, Maria? It is that girl Alice's work! Cook said she hadn't but turned her back! It is far from suitable in my opinion! It cannot be wholesome with all those currants . . . No wonder the little ones have nightmares . . .'

Then Jessie said Miss Amelia did not say any more because Miss Minchin simply pounced on her and rushed her out of the room.

And of course the pudding too.

And so Lavinia was left alone with the boy.

He stood looking out of the window and he was shaking and shaking and he laughed until he had to hold on to a chair to stop himself falling and tears were streaming down his face. So Lavinia went across to Miss Minchin's carafe and gave him a glass of water.

And he sniffed it and said, 'This is a rum school.'

Lavinia did not like that, and she told him she did not suppose he knew anything about girls' schools and he said, 'Oh yes I do. I ought to, with three sisters.'

'Three sisters?' asked Lavinia. 'Where are they, then?'

'The twins are up at Oxford,' said the boy. 'And the other one is in Sixth Form, getting ready to take her exams. She's bound to pass. Then she'll go there too.'

'To Oxford?' asked Lavinia.

The boy stuck a finger in his glass of water, licked it and grinned.

'Is it not fresh?' asked Lavinia, and then without waiting for him to answer, 'Tell me about your sisters! How old are they? Older than me? What do they study?'

'Oh,' said the boy, carrying his water glass back to the carafe and setting it down very carefully. 'What about if I just pour this back in the jug thing again? Yes? Like that? Good! My sisters? Oh, they are much older than you! Ancient! What do they study? Latin. English literature . . .'

'Oh, so do I!' said Lavinia eagerly.

'Mathematics. French. Economics. Philosophy . . .'

'Yes?' asked Lavinia, in a very little voice for Lavinia.

'. . . You know, the usual stuff . . .'

'Yes, I suppose the usual stuff,' agreed Lavinia.

'I should go now. If you happen to meet the cat . . .'

'The cat?'

'I came about the cat. He runs off. It's the piano. He can't stand the thumping. Very musical cat, Bosco.'

'Oh, Bosco!'

'My uncle has piano students, you see. They visit for lessons. More than poor old Bosco can bear. Doesn't mind the Latin and stuff. It's when they start knocking out scales . . .'

'Your uncle teaches piano?'

'Anything to earn an honest crust! I think I should see myself out. Thank you so much. Goodbye.'

And then he went, nearly falling over Jessie because he

opened the door so quickly. Lavinia ran after him calling, 'Bosco? Bosco? I won't forget. I'll keep a lookout and bring it back!'

'Him,' corrected the boy.

'Him,' agreed Lavinia, and she stood staring after the boy as he opened the front door and went away down the steps.

When she turned around (Jessie said) she had the strangest expression on her face. So Jessie assumed she had fallen in love and she was not pleased.

'I saw him first!' she protested.

'What?' asked Lavinia.

'And anyway, it's no good you liking him! You said so yourself!'

'Me?'

'It's a trap, you said!'

'A trap?' asked Lavinia, and then she seemed to shake herself awake. 'Oh you are so silly, Jess! Never mind! Come and help me! Trap! It's not a trap! It's the way out!'

Then Lavinia began emptying the hall bookcase of all those enormous encyclopaedias that Miss Minchin bought just before you left. 'Take them to my room,' she said, loading them into Jessica's arms. 'Lottie, come here! You can manage at least two. Ermengarde! Hold these!'

'Lavinia!' exclaimed Miss Minchin, arriving from nowhere while we were all piled up with books.

'May I take them to my room?' asked Lavinia. '(Go on, Jess, up the stairs, quickly!) I will look after them very carefully, Miss Minchin. (Lottie, go with Ermengarde!

Gertrude. Carry these!)'

'Lavinia, replace those books!' ordered Miss Minchin.

'Thank you so much, Miss Minchin!' said Lavinia. 'Of course, as soon as I have read them I will bring them back.' And then she said to a group of Lottie's friends who had come to see what was happening, 'All you little ones take one each!'

'Lavinia, return those books immediately!' snapped Miss Minchin.

'Yes I will, Miss Minchin,' said Lavinia, picking up the last three.

So now the bookcase in the hall is empty. Lavinia has the whole set of encyclopaedias in her room, and she has been looking up things ever since. Jessie cannot get her to talk about the red-headed boy, no matter how she tries. She is only interested in his sisters.

'But you do not know one thing about them,' complained Jessica. 'Not what they look like, or how they talk, or what they wear, or anything! Not even their names! So why are they so special?'

'Oxford,' said Lavinia.

(I truly thought only boys went to Oxford, Sara, and I think Lavinia did too, but she won't admit it.)

'Yes, but that does not make them special,' said Jessie.

'I suppose anyone can go there if they want to, and they are rich enough. I expect someone like Sara, for instance, could go right now if she liked.'

'Sara?' asked Lavinia, sounding very cross indeed. 'Sara go to Oxford? I don't think so! The boy's sisters had to pass exams! Princess Sara would have to pass them too, like everyone else.'

'Sara probably wouldn't want to go to Oxford,' said Gertrude, in a very superior kind of way. 'Oxford is only quite an ordinary town, Lavinia.'

'Ordinary?' repeated Lavinia. 'Ordinary?'

'Yes, I have been there often. It is near my home, you know. The shops are very dull. My big sister bought a hat there once, but she gave it away quite soon. My mother said afterwards that Oxford was a ridiculous place to buy a hat . . .'

'People,' said Lavinia, through her teeth, 'do not go to Oxford to buy hats.'

'Of course, there are the colleges.'

'Of course there are the colleges,' growled Lavinia. Then she went back upstairs, I expect to read more of the encyclopaedias. She had told Miss Minchin that she will bring them down one by one as she finishes them.

'There are twenty volumes. The first is A — BAN. And then BAN — CAV. And then CAV — DEL. And so on, all the way through the alphabet. The last one is XYZ.'

'By the time she finishes she will know everything,' I said to Lottie.

'Only if everything is in those books,' said Lottie.

12

Something Awful

SATURDAY AFTERNOONS, AT THE SELECT
Seminary, were entirely spent on needlework. No one
escaped. Miss Amelia embroidered hassocks, every stitch
a prayer. The little ones progressed from cross-stitched
book markers to samplers and shoe bags, while the older
girls made petticoats and cushion covers and
embroidered centrepieces. Jessica, who had a baby sister
at home, was allowed to make a baby dress. Ermengarde
laboured over a tablecloth, greyish-white, with greyish
wreaths of knotty flowers in the corners and drawn
thread work round the border. Of all the torments that
Ermengarde was forced to endure in the name of
education, she considered needlework the worst.

'Sewing machines have been *invented*,' she complained. 'I know they have! I've *seen* them! I *hate* this tablecloth! I feel like I have been making it for a hundred years!'

'You chose it,' said Gertude without pity.

'I thought it would be easy,' said Ermengarde. 'I thought it would be just flat and white. Tablecloths *should* be flat and white. Anything extra on them is a waste of time!'

For once Lavinia agreed with her.

'I am going to ask Miss Minchin if I may take piano lessons instead of sewing,' she announced. 'My mother said I could take any extras I liked, so long as someone suitable could be found to instruct me. The boy's uncle teaches music. I shall ask if he can teach me.'

'She will say no,' predicted Jessie. 'She is always so cross these days.'

'She will say yes,' said Lavinia. 'In case I leave, like Sara did. I shall go and ask straight away.'

Lavinia folded her work, tilted her sharp, pretty nose in the air and marched out of the room.

'How could Lavinia leave?' asked Gertrude, voicing what no one had dared say while Lavinia was present.

'Where would she go?'

'To her mother, of course,' said Jessica, a little defensively.

'Her mother is always away,' Gertrude pointed out. 'When you think about it, Lavvie can't have seen her for ages. Last summer she stayed with you, didn't she, Jessica?'

'Only because her mother was in France or somewhere, staying with friends.'

'And she was here at the Seminary all Christmas,' said Gertrude. 'And she never has anyone visiting, either.'

'I don't know what business that is of yours,' said Jessica, loyally.

'I was only saying that I don't think Miss Minchin need worry that she will suddenly leave,' said Gertrude, and she laughed so scornfully that Ermengarde, who had been idly pleating her tablecloth into grey ridges, suddenly felt rather sorry for Lavinia.

It seemed that Gertrude was right. Lavinia returned very soon, crashing the door open so hard that Miss Amelia awoke from her hassocky dreams to exclaim, 'Lavinia, *dear*!'

'What?' asked Lavinia rudely, and went to stand

stiffly at the window.

Glaring, thought Ermengarde, glancing sideways at her. And blinking.

Ermengarde looked away, not wanting Lavinia to see that anyone had noticed her disappointment.

After a while Lavinia stood less stiffly.

Staring, thought Ermengarde. And thinking.

She's got a plan, guessed Ermengarde, and although Lavinia was as close to an enemy as Ermengarde had ever had, she thought, I hope it works.

'Lottie!' said Lavinia, seizing her at the end of the afternoon. 'How did you get out?'

'Me?'

'Yes, you! When you posted Ermengarde's card.'

'Oh, then,' said Lottie. 'Do you want me to post something for you? I will if you like.'

'I want to get out.'

'Out the way I did?'

'Of course.'

'The gap's not big enough,' said Lottie with decision. 'Why do you want to go out, anyway?'

'I'll tell you when Ermengarde's not listening,' replied

Lavinia, her eyes fixed on something she was watching, far down in the square.

'Who's out there?' asked Lottie, inquisitively, coming over to look. 'Is it that boy from next door? I can't see anyone.'

'There isn't anyone,' said Lavinia out loud, but to Lottie she murmured, 'Come and stand where I'm standing. There, straight down!'

'Do you mean . . .' began Lottie.

'Mmmm,' said Lavinia.

'Steal?'

'Just borrow.'

'Me?'

'Well, could you?'

'Easy. Now?'

Lavinia gave her a surprised, appraising look, nodded and left the room. Lottie followed at once, and as soon as they were gone Ermengarde and Jessie and two or three others who had been listening rushed to the window.

There was no one there, except for a fat black cat sitting just within the circle of light from a street lamp. Otherwise, the square was quite empty. Presently the cat caught sight of something that interested him and sauntered away, and then there was nothing there at all.

At supper time Lottie was very naughty. She took off her shoes and poured her milk into them. In the past she had thought of a good many ways to avoid drinking her milk, but this was the worst.

'Lottie, you may leave the room at once!' snapped Miss Minchin, which Lottie did, carrying her shoes very carefully.

And that put Miss Minchin into a simply awful mood, wrote Ermengarde to Sara.

And she said after supper we would have a needlework inspection to see how we had spent the afternoon. So I rushed off to try and tidy mine up a little, but it was no use. She pounced on me straight away and that awful tablecloth I have been making for Aunt Eliza for more than a year and she said, 'What careless, disgraceful, filthy work, Miss St John! It is actually stained! Is that blood? Why is this thread all wet? I do believe you have sucked it!'

I do not know how it is possible to thread a needle without sucking the thread, Sara, and I don't believe Miss Minchin does either. But the blood did look nasty. It is only little tiny dots where I have pricked myself but there are so many of them.

'I was going to have it washed before I gave it to Aunt Eliza,' I said.

'I think your aunt would be more interested to see it as it is,' said Miss Minchin. 'You may give it to me and I will see that it is sent to her directly! Perhaps that will teach you to be more careful in future. Good heavens, girl, don't wipe your eyes with it! No wonder it is in such a dreadful state! Do you not own a handkerchief!'

And so it is gone in the post to *Aunt Eliza* all damp and dirty and I am so sorry because she is by far my nicest aunt.

Even worse, now I have six handkerchiefs to hem for *Papa*, rolled hems and his initials to go in the corners. Miss Minchin says I have to do them and they will go on *The Account.*

It has been a very nasty Saturday.

Lottie was sent up to bed early because of the milk in her shoes but she did not go quietly to sleep. We could hear her playing Zoo Animals all by herself, so loudly that Lavinia said she was going up to stop her. Gertrude went too. Lottie let Lavinia into the room, but she would not have Gertrude. She stepped out into the corridor and held the door tight shut with both hands. Gertrude tried to prise her fingers away, bending them back one at a time to make her let go.

Lottie did not let go. She bit. The tooth marks made a little circle of blue bars on Gertrude's arm. Then Lottie ran away and hid and Gertrude went shrieking for Miss Minchin and Miss Amelia.

Lottie was missing for ages. The whole school searched for her, except for Lavinia. Lavinia had come out and shut herself in her own room. Reading, I suppose. 'What a fuss!' she said, when Jessie tried to tell her what was happening, *and would not even open the door.*

The hunt for Lottie went on until quite late and I was begining to think she had slipped out of the house and been kidnapped or something awful like that. But then Alice heard snoring from behind a curtain on the landing and there she was fast asleep on that window seat where you and I used to sit sometimes. She had her thumb in her mouth and her curls were everywhere and Alice said, 'Poor little mite. I'm glad my little sister's not dumped in such a place as this.'

(Alice is not a bit respectful about Miss Minchin's, Sara, and she is not very impressed with London either. She says she only came to London to see the sights, and she says she has certainly seen some since she got here.)

Miss Amelia saw we had found Lottie and came panting up to us going, 'Hush, hush, hush!' with her finger on her lips.

'Do not wake her up,' she said. 'I simply cannot deal with another scene tonight.'

So Lottie was carried upstairs with her boots dangling and her eyes tight shut and Alice put her to bed.

'Is nothing going to be done to her?' demanded Gertrude.

'Gertrude, I have brought some arnica for your arm,' said Miss Amelia. 'And of course Lottie will be punished. But she is very young and she had never really known a proper home. She was only four when she came to us. The same age as Lavinia, actually . . . Allowances must be made, Gertrude dear! I think we should all say an extra little prayer tonight because she is safe.'

Saturdays always make Miss Amelia holier than other days, I've noticed, Sara. I suppose it is the hassock sewing, or the thought of church in the morning. Fancy, Lavinia having been here that long! I never knew. No wonder she is so bad-tempered.

I am in bed, Sara, writing this by candlelight. The house is very quiet. I think everyone must be asleep but me . . .

Oh, Sara, I have just remembered something awful!

13

Melchisedec

ERMENGARDE HAD REMEMBERED MELCHISEDEC.

'There is something very nasty about that attic,' Alice had said, and she had diagnosed Rats.

Melchisedec was a rat. A large, brown, half-tamed rat who lived in the attic. Ermengarde was not fond of him, in fact his very name made her shiver.

Melchisedec had an unpredictable way of scuttering across the floor very quickly, a pale pinkish nose, and a long hairless tail.

'I *know* he can't help his tail,' admitted Ermengarde, 'but it *isn't* nice . . .'

Melchisedec had been Sara's pet, sustained by crusts and scraps and pieces of biscuit.

But she forgot him, Ermengarde thought, and so did Lottie and I. All these weeks he has been forgotten! How long does it take, wondered Ermengarde, a horrified whimper of a wonder, for a rat to starve to death?

'I can't! I can't! I can't!' said Ermengarde, safe and warm in her bed. 'I can't go up to the attic tonight! He'll be dead. It's been more than six weeks . . .'

But even as she spoke, even as she pulled the covers right over her head and prayed to go instantly and blamelessly to sleep, her mind was busy locating the apple on her windowsill and the piece of chocolate in her pencil box. Ermengarde was a natural rescuer. She did not like Melchisedec, but she could not starve him, not now, not once she had remembered his existence.

'He's probably dead,' said Ermengarde, as she crawled out of bed. 'I'll have to arrange a funeral, I suppose. And if he's not dead, if he's still alive, I'll have to *keep on* feeding him! For ever and ever! It's not fair!'

Ermengarde had not visited the attic for a long time. She had forgotten the creaking, breathless climb up the staircase to the little ones' corridor. She had forgotten the darkness once the last light, the nightlight that burned outside the little ones' bedroom door, was passed. She had forgotten the chill that seemed to pour like water down the narrow blackness of the attic stairs.

I used to bring my shawl, remembered Ermengarde. It was another thing that she had forgotten.

There was perfect silence as she crept up the last of the attic stairs and pushed open the door.

Instantly, with a twang of rusty bed springs, something enormous leaped towards her. She gasped and waited for the impact that never came. Whatever it was hurtled past Ermengarde like a hot black ghost and disappeared down the attic stairs.

Ermengarde was frightened beyond all possibility of screaming. She had never fainted in her life, and she did not faint now, but all the same her knees gave way and she crumpled where she stood. Straight above, the full moon shook off the last of its shrouding rain clouds and glowered down through the skylight window.

And then Melchisedec the rat appeared.

One moment the room was empty, and the next he was there, hesitating among the moon shadows. Ermengarde lost her nerve completely and began to cry.

'Go away,' she begged.

Melchisedec did not go away, he came forward a little

further, but even to Ermengarde's unsympathetic eyes he moved, she thought, on tiptoe. The moonlight filled the attic room in shades of silvery-grey, but Melchisedec was not grey. He was brown and small and terrified. It was evident that he hardly dared show himself, that every hesitating movement was an act of courage, and that (after an evening spent in horrified contemplation of the enormous creature on the bed) he was quakingly aware that each step might be his last.

As he came closer to Ermengarde she could see that he was actually trembling.

'Melchisedec,' she whispered. 'That huge thing! That black thing! I think it was . . . I think it was a cat!'

He paused then, staring at her.

'A cat has come to live next door,' explained Ermengarde. 'That must have been it. I don't know how it came to be here, but you had better take care.'

He blinked, bowed with defeat at this awful news.

'Melchisedec,' murmured Ermengarde, and slid her piece of chocolate along the floor towards him.

Then Melchisedec's heart seemed to leap with joy; he pattered across to the chocolate and reached out with one paw to touch it. He stood like that for a long time, quite motionless, and his gaze met Ermengarde's as clearly and directly as any person's had ever done.

Melchisedec's eyes looked . . .

> . . . *thankful,* wrote Ermengarde. *And I was so sorry that he had been hungry and that I had forgotten him. He nibbled the chocolate very gently. I liked watching him so much that I almost forgot that I had to go back again. But when Melchisedec had finished his chocolate and gone away I knew I had to leave. I was so afraid of being heard, but I managed it, all the way down both sets of stairs and into my room.*
>
> *Only as I turned to close my door I heard Miss Minchin's voice in the hall below. She was talking to Miss Amelia.*
>
> *'There is somebody PROWLING about,' I heard her say, quite loudly and clearly, and then Miss Amelia saying, 'No, no, dear. No, no!'*

'Prowling!' repeated Miss Minchin.

'I think you should go back to bed. You should try to sleep, Maria.'

'I heard noises and footsteps! Night after night! I hear them! I cannot endure it!'

Goodness! thought Ermengarde, as she tiptoed across to her bed. I was not that noisy! And I hardly said a word! I wonder if . . . I wonder if . . . she heard the black thing . . . the cat thing . . .

It was lovely to be safe in bed. Ermengarde burrowed deep under the blankets and plugged the hole at the top with her pillow.

If it *was* a cat, she thought, doubtfully, because already it was becoming too large, too swift, too dark, too dreamlike to be completely believed in.

It may have been my imagination, she thought, and before she had time to remember that she had no imagination, she was fast asleep.

Bosco, the next door's huge, black musical cat, was curled on Lavinia's bed, and he was very glad to be there. He was exhausted. His peaceful life of sleeping and eating and avoiding music students had been totally disrupted. Since his last meal he had been captured by Lottie, posted through a basement window and smuggled into an unknown bedroom. There he had mewed and mewed and a smallish girl with sticky hands had offered him shoe-flavoured milk. Later another girl had arrived, a tall one with clean hands who stroked him respectfully. That had not been so bad, but almost immediately there had been a horrible hammering at the door. The clean-handed one had held him tightly then, while the sticky-handed little one gave chase to the hammerer.

Then there had been another smuggling, this time wrapped in someone's dressing gown.

'Poor cat,' murmured the smuggler's voice as she carried him away. 'Poor cat, never mind, you'll be all right in the morning.' And he was tipped out on to the floor.

Bosco found his feet just as he heard the door close.

Far away, voices called and footsteps ran up stairs, but Bosco was alone. He was imprisoned in a cold, damp, rat-scented attic.

This is impossible! thought Bosco.

He could not imagine why he was in such an uncomfortable situation. He did not know he was Lottie's evening adventure, and the sole reason for the milk in her shoes. Nor that in the morning he would be Lavinia's passport to the house next door, and therefore to the person who taught piano to earn an honest crust.

And maybe, dreamed Lavinia, two flights of stairs below, a beginning of much, much more.

Oxford, thought Lavinia, and remembered Gertrude's

description, and smiled, alone in the dark.

A ridiculous place to buy a hat! she told herself, and fell asleep.

Bosco was not so happy. The bed was barely adequate and the smells were very disturbing. It was a long time before he relaxed and dozed a little.

And then Ermengarde appeared in the doorway and he saw his chance to escape.

Down the stairs shot Bosco, across the landing, down another set of stairs, and through (with great good luck) the tall one's, the clean one's, Lavinia's, bedroom door.

There he spent the remainder of the night, while Melchisedec writhed in unaccustomed chocolate dreams, and the red shoes danced around Lottie's bed and Alice snored (which she never did in Epping because there the air was fresh) and Miss Minchin sipped and muttered and eventually did a little prowling herself and discovered an apple in the corridor that passed the little ones' door on the way to the attic stairs. It was Ermengarde's apple. She had dropped it when Bosco shot past her; it had rolled all the way down the stairs, and been lost.

'Ah ha!' said Miss Minchin, 'Proof!' and carried it triumphantly down and placed it on the hall table where it stood, rosy and stubborn in the lamplight, and did not quake or shiver, despite Miss Minchin's glares.

It was still there on Sunday morning when Ermengarde came down for breakfast, but by the time she passed through the hall again it had vanished. Nobody ever mentioned it, not Miss Minchin (who woke and doubted its existence) nor Ermengarde (who had disowned it) nor Alice (who ate it).

That same morning, while the school was engrossed in prayers and hair brushing and hard-boiled eggs and porridge, Lavinia boldly walked out of the door with Bosco in her arms.

She was away for a long time.

14

Sunday

SUNDAY WAS MISS AMELIA'S FAVOURITE day of the week, and the Sundays when her sister was too indisposed to attend church were the best of all.

'Of course, I would not *wish* poor Maria to feel unwell,' Miss Amelia told herself, 'especially on such a beautiful morning.'

By a beautiful morning, Miss Amelia meant nothing more than that it was not raining, and so she could walk the girls to church in a respectable manner instead of having to issue threats and warnings at every puddle. No rain also meant that she could wear her beautiful, detachable, curling grey feathers in her blue velvet hat. It would be only their second outing. The first had been in Miss Minchin's company, and Miss Minchin had not been kind. She had glared at them and sniffed and said (within hearing of the vicar too!) 'At our age, Amelia!'

As if, thought Miss Amelia, Maria was not twelve years older than I! There was a great deal of difference, Miss Amelia told herself, between almost forty-five and . . . and . . . and only just out of one's twenties!

Miss Amelia did a lot of comforting arithmetic of this kind, especially on Sundays. Once, years before, the vicar of St Stephen's had sent a basket of violets to the Select Seminary.

'A very pleasant gesture of respect to our establishment,' Miss Minchin had pronounced. Then she read the card that came with them. It was silver-edged, and embossed with leaves and flowers and addressed very clearly to *Miss Amelia Minchin* as if to emphasise that the violets were intended for Miss Amelia's pleasure alone.

Miss Minchin had taken the hint and refused to so much as sniff them. The violets had withered so quickly they might have been bewitched and the card had mysteriously disappeared from beneath Miss Amelia's pillow. The vicar was called on (twice) and told that he presumed too much (by Miss Minchin) and (by Miss Amelia) that what he dreamed could never be, but that she hoped most earnestly that they would stay friends for ever.

'And that was that,' said Miss Minchin (briskly) and Miss Amelia (anything but briskly).

Except that it wasn't that. The vicar remained unmarried and (so far as Miss Amelia could discover) refrained from sending violets to anyone else. Miss Maria developed hay fever and refused ever again to have flowers in the house, and Miss Amelia wondered every Sunday morning if she really had (as her sister assured her) made the only possible correct and virtuous decision.

Which was why she had bought the three detachable feathers for her hat, and why on Sunday morning she was so happy to assure Miss Minchin (who had a dreadful head) that of course she might stay in her room, and that she, Miss Amelia, could certainly cope with taking the Select Seminary to church.

'I don't know if *I* would call it coping,' remarked Jessica, as they all stood for the opening hymn.

'Look at the little ones!'

Lavinia and Ermengarde looked. The little ones, led by Lottie, had played a furtive game of tag all the way to church. Now they stood in the pew in front of the big girls, barely stifling their giggles in a game of 'Pass it on'. Already they had passed on pinches, and pretend sneezes, and had just finished a chain of imaginary tears mopped with Sunday handkerchiefs.

'The red-headed boy has seen them,' whispered Jessie into Lavinia's ear. 'He is smiling! And his uncle looks terribly surprised. They are both just across the aisle! Look!'

'It is too bad,' complained Lavinia. 'However will they take any of us seriously if they see us behaving like that?'

'Who wants to be taken seriously?' asked Jessica, smiling sideways under lowered eyelashes at the red-headed boy.

'I do!' Lavinia snapped, and bending towards Lottie hissed, '*Stop it!*' and jabbed her hard with the corner of her prayer book.

Lottie turned round, stuck out her tongue, and then turned back to her friends.

'Pass this on!' she whispered, and began an elaborate

mime of washing her face with licked paws, like a cat.

'They will think we are ridiculous!' Lavinia said bitterly. 'Why doesn't Miss Amelia see them? Oh, thank goodness!'

Ermengarde had belatedly remembered her promise to take care of Lottie and keep her out of trouble. Under the cover of the noise of the congregation sitting down she extracted her birthday frog and pushed it into Lottie's hands.

'Hold him carefully and be *good*!' she ordered.

'Ermie's spoiled it!' sighed Jessica. 'Oh well. I brought a storybook for the sermon. Do you think I dare?'

'You probably *dare*,' said Lavinia, dropping primly her knees to pray, 'but whether you should is another matter. Shush!'

Jessie sighed but shushed while Lavinia became absorbed in her prayer book, recently re-covered, Jessie suddenly noticed, in plain brown paper.

'Why have you . . .' she whispered. 'What have you . . . *what is that*?'

'Latin.'

'*Latin*?'

'I am teaching myself Latin,' murmured Lavinia.

'I began earlier this morning.'

'Did Miss Minchin say you must?'

'Miss Minchin has nothing to do with the matter.'

The rest of the service passed very peacefully, which did not please everyone.

'Why did you make Lottie behave in church?' Gertrude asked Ermengarde over their Sunday boiled beef and cabbage.

'Somebody had to,' said Ermengarde, rather primly.

'Really!' said Gertrude. 'You're not the new Princess Sara, you know! You needn't pretend to be so perfectly perfect, need she, Lavvie?'

'Shut up, creature!' said Lavinia, and passed Ermengarde the potatoes. Ermengarde was so astonished that she took three, even though boiled potatoes (with little black lumps where Alice's peeling had been too slapdash) were one of her least favourite foods. The sight of them on her plate was slightly dismaying and it was with some difficulty that she smuggled them, one by one, under the table. However, during the wait for apple pudding (also boiled) she managed to conceal them in her handkerchief and this cheered her up. Rats, she supposed, ate potatoes when they could not get anything better.

Later that afternoon she took them up to the attic and hid them under the bed for Melchisedec to find. The attic was a less scary place in daylight, although no less dismal. It was hard to believe, thought Ermengarde, gazing around, that Sara had lived there for so long.

'There is not one trace of her left,' she whispered, and then she spotted something she had not noticed before.

Sara's old blue cloak, the one she had worn through so many cold days and nights, still hung behind the door. Seeing it there was astonishing: it was like catching a glimpse of her lost friend in the distance, or hearing her voice from somewhere very far away.

Very gently Ermengarde lifted it down and when she left the attic she took it with her.

15

Blue Cloak

THERE WAS A LETTER FOR ERMENGARDE in the Monday morning post. It came from Sara. Miss Minchin, who laid out the pupils' letters every morning on the hall table, recognised the handwriting immediately and gave it the same withering look that she had once bestowed on Miss Amelia's violets.

'The postmark is indecipherable,' she said, as if it was Sara's fault.

'I believe they are on the south coast, dear,' said Miss Amelia.

'So we have been told,' said Miss Minchin. 'Good heavens! What is that ridiculous girl thinking of?'

She had just caught sight of Alice, who was on her way

to the dining room carrying a tray piled high with breakfast: plates of thick bread and butter, a dish of very small sausages and a huge vat of stewed apple. Even as Miss Minchin spoke an avalanche of sausages began to cascade to the floor.

'I knew that would happen!' scolded Miss Minchin. 'You foolish girl! That tray was piled far too high!'

'Never you worry!' said Alice, retrieving the sausages with perfect cheerfulness, wiping them on her apron, repositioning them on their dish and licking her fingers. 'We must all eat a peck of dirt before we die, and besides I done this floor only Friday.'

'Take those sausages back to the kitchen *instantly*!' ordered Miss Minchin, while Miss Amelia exclaimed, 'Friday! Really, Alice! First thing in the morning *every* day, if you please!'

'There'd never be time,' said Alice. 'And those sausages are counted! One each and no extras and that's all there is cooked!'

'Alice, you may go at once!' snapped Miss Minchin.

'And, Alice,' added Miss Amelia. 'The last maid managed to find time to clean the floors every day, and you must do the same.'

'The last maid,' said Alice, "as 'opped it. Which I may *also* do the same! And meanwhile I will get back to the kitchen and sort these sausages before they are stone cold.'

'That girl,' pronounced Miss Minchin, after Alice had gone, 'actually *flounces!*'

'I'm afraid she does,' said Miss Amelia.

'We must do something about it.'

'Of course we must,' agreed Miss Amelia, but all the same, when Alice (still flouncing) reappeared soon afterwards with the very same sausages, slightly rearranged and cooling rapidly, they both pretended not to notice.

'Appearances must be maintained,' said Alice, tickling Lottie under her chin with a slightly sausagey finger when they met in the hall outside. 'Good morning to you, young lady, and kindly take your boots off next time you go bouncing on my bed!'

'Oh! How did . . .'

'Footprints,' said Alice. 'Look, the letters are out! Run and tell Miss Ermengarde there's one for her. No! Don't take it to her. Let her get it herself. That's half the fun.'

'It rattles,' Lottie discovered. She departed to fetch

Ermengarde in great excitement and insisted on being present when it was opened.

The rattle (much to Lottie's disappointment: she had waited, cupped hands, for a shower of diamonds) turned out to be shells. A miniature collection of fans and whirls and silvery petal shapes.

I wanted to show you how pretty they are . . . wrote Sara, and:

. . . I have drawn you a map of my walk around the harbour and:

. . . Your postcard made me laugh and it made me a little sad too. I suddenly remembered the Sunday letter writing so clearly, and how you used to hate it!
Did you read the book? I sent it because it has a story in that I read one evening to the little ones, that last term, just before I left. You were there, and you said you wanted to hear the end, but somehow you never did. Perhaps you have forgotten . . .

I haven't, thought Ermengarde. That was the night when you would not let me visit. I haven't forgotten.

Tell Lottie I think of her often . . .

'Often?' said Lottie. 'Good!'

'I must say,' remarked Lavinia, when later in the day she heard this message, 'I don't think that was *very* sincerely meant.'

'Absence makes the heart grow fonder,' said Jessica, giggling.

'You are all just jealous,' said Lottie.

'Jealous of what?' asked Lavinia. 'What has Sara got that we haven't, Lottie dear? Besides stupendous unlimited wealth?'

'She has a stupendous unlimited boar hound with a gold and silver collar,' suggested Gertrude.

'So she does!'

'And a stupendous unlimited monkey with red trousers!'

'Well,' said Lavinia, 'we do have Lottie. It comes to much the same.'

Lottie was very pleased with this comparison. She became very bouncy indeed and demanded that Ermengarde write back to Sara at once.

'Send another funny postcard!' she begged.

'I can't. The only postcards I have are *Views of London.*

You know they are not funny.'

'Show me!'

Ermengarde sighed, but went to her desk and fetched them for Lottie. Lottie hung over them solemnly for a while, selected Buckingham Palace, added a drawing of a frog in a crown to the royal roof, and gave it back to Ermengarde.

'Write on it that I drew the frog, and that it is the Frog Prince,' she ordered. 'Hurry up, Ermie!'

'Oh, all right!'

'And tell her that there is a cat called Bosco living next door!'

Ermengarde groaned, but obeyed.

'Now give it to me and I will draw a picture of him.'

'No!' protested Ermengarde. 'There is hardly any room left already! What if I want to write something for myself?'

'But you write so much to Sara anyway. You are always writing!'

'Postcards are different.'

'Oh all right. I suppose I could draw Bosco on the front. Beside the frog. Go on then!'

'Thank you for the shells,' wrote Ermengarde in the

last remaining half-inch of space. 'I haven't read the book yet. Love from E.'

'And love from Lottie?' asked Lottie hopefully.

'You can write that, surely?'

'And love from Lottie,' wrote Lottie. 'Shall I do Bosco sitting down or standing up? Sitting? Standing? Sitting? Standing? Choose, Ermie!'

'Standing.'

'No. Sitting. Less legs! There! Now give me a stamp and I'll post it for you.'

'No,' said Ermengarde firmly. 'We will put it on the hall table and Alice will take it after it has been checked. You mustn't keep going out, Lottie! How do you do it, anyway? If you go out of the front door you must pass Miss Minchin's windows. Why does she not see you?'

'Promise never, never to tell?'

'I suppose.'

'I go out of Alice's window! She leaves it open at the top for fresh air like in Epping. I get on her bed and slide out of the gap and then I am in the basement and I can go up the steps at the side and I am free.'

'Yes, but, Lottie, you know you shouldn't.'

'It's lovely out,' said Lottie, wistfully.

And later, Sara, wrote Ermengarde, *while Miss Amelia was seeing Cook and no one was with us, she sneaked away again, even though I had told her not to. I saw her from the schoolroom window playing under the trees with Bosco. Miss Minchin was in her parlour giving Lavinia a literature lesson, and I thought any moment she would look up and see Lottie, and then Lottie would be in such trouble.*

(I am trying to look after her, Sara, like you asked, but it is very difficult.)

I could not think how to warn Lottie to move out of sight. I knew I could never get out of Alice's window myself, and if I went out by the front door Miss Minchin would recognise me at once as I passed. Even if I put on my hat or my red woolly shawl she would know it was me.

And then I suddenly remembered your old blue cloak! You forgot it, you know. You left it hanging on the attic door. I have it now.

As soon as I thought of it I knew it would be exactly right. None of the girls here at school have ever worn anything like it (I am sorry if that sounds rude, Sara, but I expect you know it is true). I could put it on and blend in straight away with the people outside, the servants or the shop girls or anyone from the little houses at the back of the square. If I put the hood up I could walk right under Miss Minchin's nose in it if I wanted.

But I didn't risk that. I just put it on very quietly and slipped outside and along the street. I got out of sight of the school and then I called Lottie over and told her she must come in at once. And then I walked right round the square before I came back inside.

And nobody noticed a thing.

Lottie is right.

It is lovely out.

A few minutes after I got back Lottie reappeared in the schoolroom. She brought Bosco with her.

Bosco likes Lottie. She told us that she had tamed him with sausage and then it turned out that quite a lot of people had sausages saved from breakfast (which they were planning to get rid of in the schoolroom fire when everyone was out of the way). So Bosco was very useful. He ate them all up. He was chewing up the last of them when Miss Amelia came in.

'He just appeared, Miss Amelia,' said Jessie at once (and I suppose that was true, although the whole truth would have been that he just appeared wrapped in Lottie's pinafore and held tight in her arms).

'Cats do just appear!' Gertrude agreed. 'We have two at home and we have a joke that they can walk through walls.'

'I don't know what my sister would say if she saw him,' said Miss Amelia nervously, but she rubbed Bosco under his chin and called him 'Poor Pussy'.

'I once had a kitten,' she said.

Everyone was sorry when Alice was told to take Bosco home, and when Lavinia heard later that she had missed seeing him, she was very grumpy indeed.

'You might have fetched me,' she said.

She had missed him because she had not come into the

schoolroom after her literature lesson. Instead she had gone upstairs to read encyclopaedias. That is what she does all the time now, when she is not teaching herself Latin. Gertrude and Jessie say she is no fun any more. I do not remember her ever being very much fun, Sara, but she has certainly become very bad-tempered since that red-haired boy said what a rum school this was.

Lavinia told us that she asked Miss Minchin again about piano lessons today. Miss Minchin told Lavinia that she must wait for her mother's written permission. Lavinia says she knows why. I am afraid that she says it is your fault, Sara. She thinks Miss Minchin does not want to be left with another set of bills that might never be paid, like she was when your papa died.

That does seem rather hard on Lavinia though, Sara, because her mother does not write very often and she might have to wait for ages.

'I haven't time to wait for ages!' complained Lavinia. 'I have wasted too much already!'

Then, guess what, Sara? I had a wonderful idea!

16

The Wonderful Idea

ERMENGARDE'S WONDERFUL IDEA CAME at supper time, a nutritious but uninspiring meal that Miss Minchin and Miss Amelia never shared and rarely supervised.

'They go off and have chicken and omelettes and things in private,' said Jessie. 'How I hate Savoury Pudding! If it is tapioca for afterwards I shall lie on the floor and scream like Lottie!'

'I don't any more,' said Lottie.

'You did only last week when it was barley soup!'

'Well, *barley soup*!' said Lottie. 'And anyway it worked. Alice made me egg-in-a-cup instead. Like they have in Epping. Sometimes you *have* to lie on the floor and scream. You won't need to tonight though, Jessie, because it's cake for afterwards.'

'How do you know? What sort of cake?'

'Alice told me. Slab cake, she said. Lavinia?'

'Mmmm?' asked Lavinia, who was reading under the table and ignoring everyone.

'Why don't you lie on the floor and scream for piano lessons?'

'I may,' said Lavinia absently, 'if I can't make Miss Minchin give in any other way,' and she turned another page in her book.

It was the book that gave Ermengarde her wonderful idea.

'You should teach yourself to play the piano!' she exclaimed.

'What?' asked Lavinia.

'Teach yourself! If you can teach yourself Latin I am sure you could teach yourself music!'

'You don't understand,' said Lavinia gloomily. 'There would be no point. I don't really . . . Oh, Alice! What's that?'

'Ginger slab,' said Alice, barging in and banging it down. 'It would go down better with custard if you ask me, but I have no say in the cooking. What did you think of that Savoury Pudding, then?'

'Awful.'

'That's what I said, but Cook doesn't agree. It only takes a couple of onions, she says, and uses up all the crusts . . . There's raisins in the slab. Pick them out if you don't like them. You're all looking very solemn then! What's it about?'

'Music,' said Jessie.

'Beyond me to understand what anyone sees in it,' said Alice, and banged out of the room again.

From the little music that Ermengarde had heard in her life, it was beyond her to see what anyone saw in it also, but she wasn't going to let her wonderful idea go because of that.

'I don't see why you shouldn't begin by teaching yourself,' she said to Lavinia. 'It would save you wasting time while you wait to hear from your mother, and it would prove to Miss Minchin how much you wanted to learn. There's a piano in the schoolroom, after all.'

'So there is,' agreed Jessica, suddenly excited. 'I'd forgotten! And I can start you off, Lavvie! I know a tune!'

'What, that you can actually play?' demanded Lavinia incredulously.

'Yes,' said Jessie, 'I do, I promise I do! Hurry up and finish and I'll show you!'

There was quite a scrabble to dispose of cake after that, chunks were pushed into pockets, Gertude, whose turn it was, gabbled through Grace even more quickly than usual, Ermengarde collected a handful of picked out raisins for Melchisedec, and they all rushed back to the schoolroom.

The Miss Minchins' piano had been overlooked for years, pushed into a corner, covered with a huge piece of dark cloth, and piled high with clutter. Jessica wasted no time, unloading old books, cases of dried flowers and cardboard missionary boxes. The covering cloth was pulled away in a cloud of dust.

Then Jessica fetched a chair, lifted the lid, trod firmly on the loud pedal, and began to play.

Everyone was very much astonished.

'What on earth is it?' asked Lavinia.

'It is called "Chopsticks",' said Jessie, 'and it is as easy as pie.'

'Play it again!'

Jessica did. And again. And again.

'It is astonishing,' said Lavinia. 'Why does it sound like that? Is it because the piano is out of tune, or do you keep hitting wrong notes? Can you teach me?'

'Not if you are going to be so horrible,' said Jessica.

'I'm not,' said Lavinia. 'I'm really not! I'd love to be able to do it. Please play it again, Jessie!'

So Jessica did, and across the hall from the schoolroom Miss Minchin's door opened.

There followed an evening of very hard work. Jessica taught Lavinia to play 'Chopsticks' and Lavinia almost learned. She practised and practised until Jessica said, 'There are other tunes you might play.'

'No,' said Lavinia. 'This is the one for me!' and she began it all over again.

If it had been anyone but Lavinia there would have been a rebellion. As it was, people simply went to bed. When Miss Amelia arrived to check on the little ones she found the schoolroom nearly empty. There was no one there except Lavinia and Jessica, and Ermengarde, who was huddled up on a window seat, putting off the moment when she would have to visit Melchisedec in the attic.

'Listen, Miss Amelia!' said Jessica. 'I have taught Lavvie a tune!'

'Yes, I have been having a music lesson,' added Lavinia. 'Won't Miss Minchin be pleased that I have managed to make a start. It seemed such a waste of time to wait until we heard from my mother . . .'

'Yes, dear, we did hear your playing,' said Miss Amelia. 'It was extremely loud.'

'I think it must be a very good piano,' agreed Lavinia.

'And it has gone on for some considerable time . . .'

'Oh, but I had all my lessons finished,' Lavinia assured her. 'And so had Jessie. You need not worry about that. And I have studied my extra literature too, and learned the battle speech from *Henry V* and written out my *Hamlet* essay.'

In the hall behind Miss Amelia, Ermengarde glimpsed the shadowy presence of Miss Minchin standing in the parlour doorway. Lavinia did not seem to notice, however. She continued to discuss Shakespeare in her confident, clear voice.

'. . . The subject was how Ophelia could have influenced the fate of the Royal House of Denmark by the application of logic and the rejection of the overemotional arguments put forward by her cousin. (Hamlet. The prince.) I have written seven pages with botanical footnotes. I hope Miss Minchin will be pleased. Should you like me to read it to you, Miss Amelia?'

Miss Amelia said she thought not and retreated very hastily, quite forgetting her orders to lock up the piano and remove the key. Lavinia locked it herself (after one more triumphant rendering of 'Chopsticks'), pocketed the key, and hurried upstairs to learn Latin in bed.

Jessica and Ermengarde followed, neither of them being very keen to stay in the schoolroom alone.

'Sara used to though,' pointed out Ermengarde.

'She used to sleep in the attic too,' said Jessica. 'I don't know how she could bear it. Alice says there's rats up there. Do you think that's true, Ermie?'

'I suppose it might be,' admitted Ermengarde, plodding up the stairs beside Jessica.

'Do you think Sara knew?'

'Perhaps.'

'Do you know what, Ermie, I thought I saw Sara, crossing the square yesterday. You know how she used to wear that awful blue— Oh!'

Jessica clutched Ermengarde's arm so tightly that

Ermengarde squealed and at the same moment Miss Minchin rose slowly up from the staircase window seat.

'Oh, Miss Minchin! You startled me!' gasped Jessica.

Miss Minchin said, 'You were talking about Sara Crewe.'

'Yes,' admitted Jessica. 'Yes, yes we were.'

'But for me she would have starved in the streets,' said Miss Minchin.

Then she passed between them and disappeared down the stairs before either of them thought of a single word to say.

Melchisedec the rat seemed to have made up his mind to like Ermengarde. He actually came out of his hole to meet her when she tiptoed up with her supply of ginger cake and raisins. Perhaps it was just hunger, perhaps the old blue cloak that Ermengarde wore deceived him, and he thought that she was Sara come back, but he ran right into the circle of candlelight and sat there quite comfortably, nibbling raisins and watching her with his jewel-black eyes. His cold potatoes had all vanished, and they seemed to have done him good. He was fatter already, and his fur was sleek and glossy.

'You look much better, Melchisedec,' Ermengarde told him. 'I'm sorry I forgot you for so long.'

Melchisedec stopped nibbling and turned to look at her, his ears pricked, his front paws dangling.

'I think you almost understand,' said Ermengarde, smiling a little. 'I wonder if you do. Sara used to think so. She used to say that you could not help being a rat. No one asked you if you'd rather be a sparrow, or a person. Just like I can't help being Ermengarde, and Lavinia can't help being Lavinia. And Sara, I suppose, couldn't help being Sara.'

Ermengarde gazed around the forlorn, candlelit attic and tried to remember how once it had appeared as a magical glowing little paradise.

It was like remembering a dream.

'It's gone,' she said. 'It was here and it vanished. You must have seen it, Melchisedec. Did it feel real to you? Truly real? Do you think it ever felt truly real to Sara? Perhaps it never quite did.'

Melchisedec looked steadily up at her, a most humorous, kind, understanding expression on his face.

'You are a very good rat,' said Ermengarde, and reached out a gentle finger and touched him very lightly.

17

Lavinia

LAVINIA WROTE TO HER MOTHER TO ASK permission to take music lessons at the house next door and the whole school waited for the reply.

'Which is silly,' said Lavinia, 'because she is in France and French post takes ages. Weeks, usually.'

'Oh no, Lavinia, it doesn't,' said Gertrude tactlessly. 'I only wish it did! I know because my godmother in Paris writes nearly every week to me. Pages and pages of dreary stuff, full of questions that she makes me reply to in French.'

'I don't see how she *can* make you,' remarked Ermengarde. 'No one could make me reply to them in French! I don't know enough French words for one thing!'

'I look them up in the dictionary,' explained Gertrude. 'I have to, it's only sensible. She's very rich, and she has no children, you see. She's old, too (although she always sounds dreadfully healthy in her letters) . . .'

'*Gertrude!* The poor old lady!' exclaimed Jessica.

'What? She's not poor! And anyway, I was only explaining to Lavinia that French post doesn't take weeks!'

'Well, it sounded awful the way you said it. And besides, French post does sometimes take weeks. Lavinia only just heard from her mother about the photograph she sent ages ago, before Christmas.'

Jessica was only trying to stick up for Lavinia, wrote Ermengarde, in one of her enormous letters to Sara, *but it made Lavinia very cross to be reminded about that photograph. You saw it, Sara, do you remember? Lavinia wore a lace blouse and her hair was rolled up on the back of her head and she looked so grown up, half smiling and half thinking. (A little bit scornful too.)*

Lavinia was very proud of that picture.

When you saw it you said, 'That isn't what Lavinia looks like yet, not really. But in ten years' time, it will be true.'

But you were wrong, Sara, it did not take ten years or even five. It just took the red-headed boy next door to say what a rum school this was. Because Lavinia looks like that all the time now and her mother will not be pleased when she sees her again. Everyone heard what she wrote in the letter back to Lavinia after she had the photograph because Lavvie screwed it up and threw it across the room, and after she had gone Gertrude unscrewed it and read it to us. I know I shouldn't have listened, but I did and Gertrude read it in such a funny voice that I laughed too.

'My friends over here would be shocked if they saw you looking like that!' Lavinia's mother wrote. 'Why, many of them (one silly darling man in particular) cannot believe I am old enough to have a little daughter at school at all! So send another one, sweetheart, with your hair down and your lovely smile. I so want to show him my precious little moppet . . .'

No wonder Lavinia was furious, Sara! Oh, I do hope her mother writes back soon about the piano lessons, because the sound of her practising is simply . . .

'Awful,' moaned Jessica. 'Her mother really ought to say "Yes". Lavinia *needs* piano lessons!'

That seemed to be the truth. Lavinia practised and practised, early in the mornings, straight after lunch, half the evenings, but she never seemed to improve. She practised with her Latin or history or maths propped up on the music rack and the loud pedal down and the schoolroom door wide open.

It went on for a week.

'If it was any other girl . . .' Miss Amelia lamented, but it was not any other girl, it was Lavinia, star pupil, unchallenged leader, and Miss Minchin's secret pride.

Lavinia was fighting a battle.

'I must,' she said, grimly, dragging open the piano lid and settling down for another frightful session. 'I must make Miss Minchin understand how important this is.'

'You would think your life depended on you having piano lessons,' complained Gertrude.

'It does,' said Lavinia.

Night after night the little ones retreated early to bed and Alice talked of Epping and Jessica and Ermengarde were reproached for their part in the torment. Miss Minchin hardly slept during that nerve-jangling time. She prowled and sipped and pressed her fingers to the sides of her aching head until on Friday afternoon Alice decided enough was enough and marched into the parlour and took charge.

'What you need to do,' Alice told her, 'is fling that dratted piano out into the street before it does for us all. One more day of it and I shall take off back to Epping and then where will you be? Never tell me you could cope because I know better and if you don't mind me saying you look shocking, Miss.'

Miss Minchin seemed hardly to hear.

'Hmmm,' said Alice and got to work and ten minutes later Miss Minchin found herself tucked up on the sofa, with her shoes off and the curtains drawn, the fire made up and the decanter filled with fresh water.

'Get your head down,' commanded Alice, and shut the door.

Miss Minchin slept for hours and hours while the whole school, under Alice's supervision, played tag and catch-the-ball under the leafless plane trees of the square. Miss Amelia found this very hard to endure. She stood on the doorstep and wrung her hands and worried about what the neighbours would think of a Select Seminary that played gutter games in the street.

'How nice it has been to see your little flock enjoying themselves so much,' said the vicar, pausing to nod and smile at the end of that undignified afternoon. 'How they chatter! Charming!'

'Oh!' said Miss Amelia, with a great sigh of relief, and

stopped wringing her hands and smiled instead, and even went so far as to suggest that the weather was quite pleasant and might make one think of spring.

'Of course you must think of spring,' the vicar told her. 'Ah, here come the girls! And Alice, I believe!'

'Yes, Alice,' agreed Miss Amelia, and remembering how Alice had saved her from the suet and many other equally appalling tasks, surprised herself by adding, 'a treasure.'

The vicar raised his hat to Alice and beamed and stood aside as the girls began clattering up the steps, past the brass plate, and through the front door of the Select Seminary.

'It was lovely!' said Lottie, staggering up with Bosco in her arms.

'Next time we will bring skipping ropes,' promised Alice, bobbing to the vicar and at the same time glancing at his unpolished shoes and old black hat. 'Good afternoon, sir, you want to take a good stiff brush to that hat, if you'll pardon me mentioning it. Bring up the nap! Miss Ermengarde, you will need to take those boots off before you take a step inside! Lottie, I hope I didn't just see you lick that cat!'

'He licked me first,' said Lottie.

'Nevertheless, Alice is right. You must not lick cats, my dear,' the vicar told her solemnly.

'But I love him!'

'I did not say you might not do that,' said the vicar. 'Love, by all means! Yes, indeed! We all have that privilege . . . Good afternoon, girls! Alice! Good afternoon, Miss Amelia.'

The afternoon did them all good.

'Lavinia, I have made arrangements,' announced Miss Minchin that evening. 'The gentleman next door will take you for a music lesson every day from four to five. He appeared to think you have great potential. It seems you have already met?'

'I took back his cat,' explained Lavinia.

'He is of the opinion that you deserve every chance to further your education.'

'Did he say that?' asked Lavinia, eagerly. 'Actually that, Miss Minchin?'

'Those were his words. He also very kindly said that you may practise over there for as long as you feel you need.'

'Oh, Miss Minchin!' exclaimed Lavinia, suddenly flushing with relief. 'Oh, thank you, thank you!'

'He tells me that he believes very strongly in the education of young women in whatever talents they happen to possess.'

Lavinia breathed deeply, like a person breathing a new air.

'. . . As, of course, do I . . .'

Miss Minchin paused for quite a long time then, perhaps remembering her own youth, when no one she knew believed that young women had any need for education at all.

'I told him about you,' said Lavinia. 'I told him how you helped me, and about the English literature classes I have with you. He said I was very fortunate.'

'Shakespeare,' said Miss Minchin, pressing her temples in the way she so often did lately, 'is everything.'

'Yes, Miss Minchin,' Lavinia agreed with unusual gentleness. 'Almost.'

18

Night Watch

THE HOUSE, WITHOUT LAVINIA'S PIANO practising, felt strangely quiet.

'Not at night,' said Lottie, who had not forgotten the story of the red shoes. 'At night I hear things.'

Ermengarde also heard things at night. A creak on a stair when the house should be asleep. A rustle in the air as she tiptoed, in Sara's old blue cloak, up to the attic to feed the ever hungry Melchisedec.

'Sparrows,' said Alice robustly, when they went to her for comfort. 'Sparrows, rats, wind in the chimneys and them next door.' Alice had taken a great dislike to the people next door ever since the red-headed boy, on seeing her rubbing at the brass plate early one morning, had enquired cheerfully, 'Polishing up the Pudding Shop?' Alice had retaliated by hurling her polishing cloth at his grinning head, declaring war on his cat, and condemning him to death.

Alice says the boy next door is not long for this world, Ermengarde wrote to Sara.

She says it is as plain as plain for those that have the eyes to see. Her cousin in Epping had just the same look, they all knew he would die, and he did. He fell under a hay cart outside the Epping Arms.

'Oh really, Alice!' exclaimed Lavinia, when she heard this. 'What awful rubbish! How could you have seen that someone would fall under a hay cart outside the Epping Arms?'

This aggravated Alice.

'Well, Miss Marvellous,' she said, 'I will tell you how we knew and that is his corpse candle. Which had been seen down the High Street and all the way to church for weeks previous and as far out of town as the blacksmith's on the turnpike, too!'

A corpse candle, Alice explained, is a little light that bobs along in the night along the path that your coffin will take.

'Is it geographically accurate?' asked Lavinia. 'Did your cousin's coffin travel down the High Street and as far out of town as the blacksmith's on the turnpike? I have never been to Epping but it sounds the long way round.'

'If it is your own corpse candle you will see your face in it,'

said Alice, glaring at Lavinia. 'Like a little glowing reflection and then you know you will shortly die.'

'Of fright,' said Gertrude.

(I am sure she is right.)

'It's a good thing the little ones are in bed,' said Jessie, and she moved very close to Lavinia.

'Pooh!' said Lavinia. 'Old wives' tales!'

So Alice showed us approximately what a corpse candle would look like by turning out the schoolroom gas and holding a candle very close to her face under her chin and rolling her eyes back upwards until only the white part showed.

Most of us screamed, but Lavinia snorted and she said she thought the boy next door need not worry, as the Epping Arms was a good way off and hay carts not frequent in London in February.

'Hay carts have nothing to do with the matter!' said Alice, now very cross indeed. 'He would have died of his chest anyway. It was bound to be. Ask anyone (in Epping).'

And then she flounced out and we discovered Lottie had been on the window seat behind the curtain listening to every word. She was all upset.

'I am tired of people dying,' said Lottie. 'Mamma, and Sara, and now the boy next door.'

'You know perfectly well that Sara is not dead,' said Lavinia.

'Well, she might as well be,' said Lottie, all teary and messy, 'she's gone, hasn't she?'

(It's true. You have, Sara.)

'Nothing is the same any more,' said Lottie.
(Poor little Lottie. It is sad when you realise that.)
'I want Bosco,' said Lottie.
'He is probably safe in bed,' I told her.
'He's not,' said Lottie. 'He's out there by the street lamp. Will you get him for me, Ermie?'
'No,' I said. 'How could I? It's dark, don't be silly.'
So she cried a lot more.

I almost got caught opening the front door. I just managed to whisk outside as I heard someone come into the hall. Bosco came running up as soon as he saw me, though. Bosco loves Miss Minchin's, and no wonder! Lottie and her friends have been stuffing him all week with bacon rind and boiled cod and macaroni cheese. So it was as easy as anything to scoop him up and carry him inside. And Lottie was very pleased. She took him to bed with her. Lavinia says I ought not to let her, but I don't see why not. The other little girls won't be disturbed, they are all fast asleep. Lottie can cuddle Bosco until she feels better, and when it is much later I will creep upstairs and fetch him and slip him outside again. I am getting used to this house at night, Sara, and I am trying to look after Lottie, like I promised I would.

I am in bed now, Sara, sitting up wrapped in my red shawl writing this letter to you. I know that next door to me Lavinia is also awake. I can hear the creaking of her bed, and the pages turning in whatever book she is reading. That is how quiet it is . . .

It was no use, no matter how hard she tried, Ermengarde's eyes would not stay open. She closed them for a moment and was immediately engulfed in a delicious tumble of sleep.

19

Early Morning

HOURS LATER LOTTIE AWOKE TO FIND
somebody walking in tight urgent circles on her chest. It
was Bosco, doing his utmost to make her understand
that he must go outside at once.

'Lie down, Bosco! Go back to sleep!' murmured
Lottie. 'It's hours yet till morning!'

But Bosco did not lie down. He scrabbled at the covers
and mewed and as plainly as he could he informed Lottie
that he could stay with her no longer.

'All right, all right!' whispered Lottie. 'I'm coming!
Shush!'

Bosco, seeing that he had succeeded in getting what
he wanted, obediently shushed. Lottie clambered out of

bed, pulled on her woolly bedtime wrap, scooped Bosco under one arm, picked up her shoes and stockings, and tiptoed out of the door.

At once she saw that she had been wrong to suppose that it was still night. A greyness was seeping around the heavy landing curtains and the little nightlight candle in its saucer of water had burned out into a sooty puddle of wax. It was very early morning.

And I have it all to myself! rejoiced Lottie, hugging Bosco with glee, and she set off through the sleeping house, tiptoeing barefoot past the silent doorways and then making her way stealthily down the stairs. From the hall came the sound of the ticking of the grandfather clock. It seemed far louder than it usually did, just as the stairs seemed longer, and the closed doors more firmly shut.

Everything, thought Lottie, is louder or taller or darker or stronger! Bosco is heavier, even . . . Oh!

She had arrived in the entrance hall and discovered the front door standing wide open.

Bosco leaped from her arms and vanished into the morning.

Lottie ran after him and then stopped in surprise.

There, kneeling on the doorstep, was Alice, her sleeves rolled up and her hair all in a tumble down her neck, just as it had fallen on the afternoon when she had taught the Select Seminary to play tag.

'Dratted cat!' said Alice.

'Alice!' exclaimed Lottie, with pleasure. 'What *are* you doing here?'

'I might ask the same of you,' said Alice.

'I just woke up,' said Lottie vaguely, seeing that Bosco was nowhere in sight. 'What has happened to your hair? Have you been playing? Can I play as well?'

'You can turn right round and go back to bed,' said Alice. 'And nothing has happened to my hair, thank you very much! I just haven't had time. And kindly stop paddling your bare feet on my clean step!'

'You've been scrubbing it,' said Lottie, spotting a bucket.

'I have.'

'Why?'

'What do you mean, why?'

'Was there something awful on it?' asked Lottie hopefully. 'Blood or something?'

'I never heard the like!' said Alice.

'Shall I help you?' offered Lottie, sitting on the doorstep and struggling into her stockings with a delicious feeling of adventure. 'I've brought my boots and everything. Is it an Epping thing to do, scrubbing?'

Alice suddenly stopped glaring and laughed.

'Look around you,' she said.

Lottie obediently craned her neck to inspect herself, the back of her woolly wrap, the hem of her nightgown, her boots.

'I meant look around the *square*,' said Alice.

'Goodness!' said Lottie, looking.

Clearly scrubbing was not an Epping thing, because there on the front steps of nearly every house, was a little grey shape. A kneeling figure with sleep-tangled hair, a bucket and a brush, each of them scrubbing at the doorsteps with varying amounts of energy and sloppy water.

'Oh, let me scrub too!' begged Lottie, absolutely enchanted. 'I never have before! Please, Alice! Just one step! I'll be very careful!'

'In this wind? With no coat nor nothing?'

'It's boiling hot! I've got my woolly thing. Anyway, the others are doing it in this wind without coats.

Not even shawls, some of them. Oh, now what are you doing?'

'I am whitening up with a donkey stone,' said Alice. 'So called, before you ask, because it has a picture of a donkey stamped on it which you can't see because it's all rubbed off. On account, young lady, of these steps being done every morning, including Sundays, dirty or not, snow or shine, while rich folks are in bed. Where you should be. Go on then, you can have a rub down there at the bottom, and if you make marks on my clean steps I'll snickersneeze you, so be warned!'

That morning was the start of a whole new interest for Lottie. What other pleasures, she wondered, did Alice privately enjoy while she, Lottie, lay boringly asleep, or dozed over dreary lessons, or played and squabbled by the schoolroom fire?

She soon found out.

'Get out of here this minute!' said Alice in the candlelit coal cellar, streaked with black from head to foot and wielding a hammer.

'I will, I will! Only let me watch for a moment! You *are* lucky, Alice! Are you allowed to come here and do it whenever you like?'

'Do what whenever I like?'

'Bang the coal with that hammer.'

'Bang it?' asked Alice.

'Well, you did just now! I saw you.'

'You saw me *splitting* the coal,' said Alice. 'Splitting it, Miss Nosy Parker, because this is Best Coal which comes in great lumps, too big for the kitchen range, never mind the scuttles. And if either of them upstairs had to do this job for an hour they would order Second Best in future and put up with the dust.'

Lottie did not even bother to wonder what on earth Alice could be talking about because just then she raised her hammer again.

'Stand back!' said Alice, and gave an enormous lump of coal such a wallop that the candlelight flickered and a trickle of grey plaster dust fell from the ceiling and the lump split from top to bottom into two beautiful flat halves.

'There's something in it! There's something in it!' shrieked Lottie, and sure enough, there on one of the newly split sides was a print of a leaf, a perfect fern leaf, spread out like fragile grey lace against the black.

'There are sometimes patterns,' admitted Alice begrudgingly.

'Where do they come from?'

'Long ago, I reckon.'

'A hundred years?'

'More'n that,' said Alice, and dropped the hammer again so that the lovely ancient shadow shattered and was gone.

'You broke it,' wailed Lottie, dropping to her knees to scrabble among the fragments.

'You have to break it,' said Alice, hauling her up again. 'It's coal. It's to be burned. I've broke dozens. There'll be another.'

Lottie continued to wail.

'There's always another. And bits that sparkle like gold sometimes, fool's gold, they call it. And once I found a little horseshoe, a pony shoe from down the pit. Come on, stop crying!'

Lottie gulped.

'That's right. Wipe your face! That pinafore's as black as black, what'll you tell Miss Amelia?'

'I'll say I was playing with the coal. She won't ask which coal. Alice . . .'

'What, then?'

'Can't I have just one tiny go with your hammer?'

Lottie learned to clean steps and to split coal. She learned to sift the ashes and sprinkle the floors with soggy tea leaves and sweep them up again into a dusty heap. She learned to wipe with anything handy the Select Seminary's not very sparkling brass plate. Alice stopped arguing about giving her a go. At home in Epping she had taught her little sisters to help; Lottie in her opinion was no different to them.

Alice's methods were very slapdash.

'And if they wasn't,' said Alice, 'I'd never get through half the work! And anyway, why should I worry? You can't buy perfect for twelve pounds a year.'

As often as not the dusty tea leaves were swept under the parlour mat. ('I'll get 'em when I remember my pan,' said Alice.) The supper cloth was turned upside down for breakfast and the teacups arranged over the stains. The boots and shoes were cleaned more often with spit-and-a-rub than blacking. In fact, spit-and-a-rub was Alice's solution to many things, fingerprints on door plates, a splodge on the hall floor, a smear on the table.

'What the eye doesn't see,' said Alice cheerfully, when she used the bread knife to slice a terrible tangle out of Lottie's curly hair, and 'Never *you* do that!' she told Lottie when she started reluctant fires with a trickle of lamp oil. The schoolroom was cleaned 'With a lick and a promise,' said Alice, whisking the litter down the back of the piano, and dusting the tables with her sleeve. Alice poked down cobwebs with Miss Amelia's umbrella, dusted the clock with Ermengarde's gloves, rubbed mutton fat into Lottie's chapped hands (which made them smell of dinner), cured warts with a holy potato and bumps with a kiss.

'Don't ever go back to Epping,' begged Lottie.

20

Music Lessons

LAVINIA WAS WORKING IN A WAY THAT
no pupil of the Select Seminary had ever done before.
Not since the days when the unsatisfactory young Maria
Minchin toiled over her brothers' school books, had
anyone worked so hard in that house. Lavinia's working
day started at first light, but it reached its peak at four
o'clock in the afternoon when she hurried next door for
her music lesson. Then at least two hours would pass
until she reappeared, speechless with learning,
staggering under piles of books. Ermengarde said it was
enough to put anyone off music for life. Jessica began to
feel that she had lost a friend and gained instead a
brown-paper-covered library.

'It's only music lessons!' she protested, when day after day Lavinia was too busy to look through magazines, or play a game, or even curl up on a window seat and talk.

'Hush, I'm working,' said Lavinia.

'*It is* only music lessons, isn't it? What are you reading *now*?'

'A play I am studying with Miss Minchin.'

'Horried old Shakespeare?'

'Mmmm. *King Lear*.'

'*Talk* about it, Lavvie!' begged Jessica, to whom even gossip about horrid old Shakespeare was better than no gossip at all. 'Was he nice?'

'Who, King Lear? No, not at all! Rather a bully, and very sorry for himself. Miss Minchin says he treated his children most unfairly. The youngest was dreadfully spoiled. Miss Minchin says that often happens.'

Lavinia looked sourly across the schoolroom at Lottie, who was sucking her fingers and humming lazily while Ermengarde struggled to help her understand her sums.

'I don't mind not knowing *how* they are done,' Lottie was saying. 'So long as they *are* done. Just write down the answers for me, Ermie, so I can copy them out.'

'Really!' exclaimed Lavinia. 'She will never learn

anything! Make her do them herself, Ermengarde!'

'She can't.'

'She must!'

'They are money sums, Lavvie,' explained Lottie. 'Take aways, too!'

'When you are grown up,' said Lavinia sternly, 'do you not think you will have to do money sums?'

'I shall make my husband do them.'

Lavinia snorted.

'Or one of the servants. Or Ermie when she comes to visit me! Do hurry up, Ermie, or I won't have any time left to play.'

'Listen to her!' said Lavinia to Jessica. 'That's being the youngest! Miss Minchin is right! Absolutely spoiled!'

'What happened to the youngest in *King Lear*?' asked Jessie.

'Died.'

'Goodness! Poor old Lottie! And to the King?'

'Went mad.'

'You should warn Miss Minchin,' said Jessica, giggling. 'Lottie looks quite healthy still, but Miss Minchin has been behaving very strangely lately.'

This remark did not please Lavinia. Since she had

been allowed to begin her piano lessons she had been oddly kind about Miss Minchin.

'It was hard for her to let me start having music lessons next door,' she said, trying to explain. 'Not just because my mother had not given permission. (She has written to Miss Minchin now, you know. She says I can have as many as I like.) It was hard for other reasons too. Miss Minchin had always taught me herself until now.'

'Not always,' objected Jessica. 'What about the dancing master, and French with Monsieur Dufarge?'

'They were employed by Miss Minchin.'

'What difference does that make?'

'It's not the same.'

Lavinia returned to her book, and Jessica, after watching her turn the pages for a few minutes, went slowly out of the room. Gertrude, who had listened in on the whole conversation, followed after Jessica a moment later.

'What nonsense Lavinia talks!' she exclaimed to Jessie. 'She thinks she is so special! As if Miss Minchin cared about any of us! She didn't want her to have extra lessons in case Lavvie's mother said she would not pay, and she changed her mind because she could not bear to hear her practising any longer. Simple!'

Even Jessie had the sense to realise that it was not really as simple as that.

'Miss Minchin does care about Lavinia,' she said loyally. 'She always has. Lavinia has been here for longer than any of us. And she really is clever! Miss Minchin has always been proud of her cleverness. That's why she gives her special English literature lessons.'

'English literature!' sniffed Gertrude. 'Shakespeare! Who cares about that?'

'Miss Minchin cares. And Lavinia does too. That's what I mean. Lavinia is more Miss Minchin's than any of the rest of us.'

Miss Minchin would have agreed with that. Lavinia was her complete success, the cool, intelligent proof of the worth of the Select Seminary. Everything in Lavinia's head (and there was, as everyone realised, a good deal in Lavinia's head) had got there by way of Miss Minchin. Not only English literature, but also old-fashioned botany (springtime after springtime daffodils had arrived at the Select Seminary to be sliced up, drawn and labelled by Lavinia under Miss Minchin's supervision), arithmetic and algebra and a huge amount of history. It was English history of course, as seen through the intolerant eyes of Miss Minchin, which meant lingering over the Romans ('Just what the country needed'), dismissing the Vikings and Saxons ('Unmannerly'), and grudgingly admiring the Normans.

'They raised the *tone* of the country,' admitted Miss Minchin.

She also approved of the Tudors ('They knew their minds') and detested the Stuarts ('Scots').

After the Tudors and Stuarts Miss Minchin skipped a good deal until she reached Victoria, the Queen of her childhood, whom she had once actually seen, and who, as far as looks went, might well have been a distant relation.

Victoria's Empire and its useful products (tea and silk especially) were the basis of all the Select Seminary's geography lessons. Indian diamonds had also once been a useful product of Empire, but in recent times neither India nor diamonds were ever mentioned. Australian Sapphires took their place whenever gemstones were needed.

This was the education that Lavinia had described to the red-headed boy and his uncle, during her very first visit, on the Sunday morning when she returned the kidnapped Bosco.

The boy's uncle politely bent his head and took notes. The boy also managed to conceal his feelings, right up until the final moment when Lavinia concluded her summary of Useful Products of Australia and came to a halt at last. 'But what about kookaburras?' asked the red-headed boy, grinning hugely at Lavinia's description of World Knowledge according to Miss Minchin, 'and Captain Cook and kangaroos and convicts?'

'Those are not exports,' said Lavinia stiffly, causing the boy to absolutely howl with laughter.

'Tristram, please leave the room,' ordered his uncle, and when he had gone he asked Lavinia, 'And that is how you have been studying, all these years?'

'I have managed as well as I can,' said Lavinia, and it was true. No one could slice and draw and analyse a daffodil as well as she, nor recite the Kings of England (with dates) at such a rattling speed, nor translate French verse so confidently. No maps were as well drawn as hers; Lavinia could outline coasts and borders, mountains and cities, rivers and ports, with the brisk efficiency of a world conqueror.

'But it is not enough,' said Lavinia.

'What do your parents say?' enquired the red-headed boy's uncle.

'My mother is in France,' said Lavinia, 'and anyway, she has other interests. My father taught me Latin before he . . . he . . .'

The red-headed boy's uncle nodded understandingly.

'*Amo, amas*,' said Lavinia, regaining her composure, 'and other things. I am sure I could learn if I tried.'

'I am sure you could too,' agreed the red-headed boy's uncle.

That was the beginning of Lavinia's astounding music lessons.

'I should love to be able to play the piano properly. Will you teach me everything you learn?' begged Jessica, which made Lavinia look very guilty indeed.

'When I have caught you up I will,' she agreed at last.

'Well, that will take hardly any time at all,' said Jessica.

'I think, Jessie,' said Lavinia truthfully, 'you will

probably always be far, far better at music than I!'

'I think so too!' remarked a voice from the schoolroom curtains, and Jessica swished them back to reveal Lottie, who had been quietly eating stolen raisins on the window seat behind.

'Lottie!' exclaimed Jessica. 'Why didn't you go to bed when the other little ones went up? And what are you doing there, anyway? Don't you know it's horrid to listen to other people's conversations!'

'I didn't listen, I just heard,' said Lottie, tucking sticky raisin stones under the window seat cushions. 'I wasn't being horrid at all! I'll tell you what's horrid! Horrid is when Lavinia plays the piano!'

'You rude child!'

'I'm only saying what everyone thinks,' said Lottie, and escaped up the stairs to bed.

'Take no notice, Lavinia,' said Jessica, when she had gone. 'She is just a silly little girl. She doesn't know anything about music. Don't be upset.'

'I'm not a bit upset,' Lavinia said airily, and looking at her Jessica could see that she was telling the truth.

'And yet, Lavinia usually *hates* criticism,' Jessica said privately to Ermengarde.

'I know,' agreed Ermengarde. 'And Lottie is right about the way she plays. It is awful! You would think if someone as clever as Lavinia had a piano lesson every day they would be wonderful after a week or so. Lavinia hardly plays any more, but when she does it sounds just like it always did.'

'Perhaps it's the piano,' suggested Jessica.

'*You* can play it,' pointed out Ermengarde, 'so that doesn't make sense.'

That was true. Jessica's playing improved every time she took it into her head to excavate the schoolroom piano from whatever had been piled on top of it. Jessica could remember every tune she had ever heard, and she found that with a little trial and error she could pick them out on the keys, sometimes with two fingers, but increasingly often with four, or even more.

'It's easy,' she told Lavinia, one Sunday afternoon when she had enticed her down to the schoolroom to listen. 'Mamma says next year when I am home all the time I can have proper lessons with my cousins.'

'Oh good,' said Lavinia absent-mindedly, turning a page of her latest brown-paper-covered book. Jessica had already had a look at that book. It was nothing to do with music.

'It's Background,' said Lavinia, very vaguely indeed.

'Background for music?'

'Background for nearly everything.'

'I hope I don't ever have to read it,' said Jessica. 'But I will love to learn the piano. Then we can play duets, Lavvie, when you come to visit me.'

'Mmmm.'

'We can take turns, who plays the treble part and who the bass. That's what my cousins do.'

'Lovely,' agreed Lavinia, not looking up.

'Lavvie, are you actually listening to anything I say?'

Recently Lavinia had acquired a pair of slim steel compasses and discovered angles and circles with undreamed of possibilities. She had met and understood the delicious logic of Latin. All the time Jessica had been talking and playing she had been reading a book that had introduced to her astonished mind the concept of evolution for the very first time.

But also she had been listening to Jessica.

'Duets,' she said. 'Like your cousins. At your house, when I visit. After you have learned to play the piano.'

'We can give little concerts,' said Jessica. 'What's the

matter, Lavinia? Why are you laughing like that? What did I say that was so funny? Oh, *don't* start reading again!'

It was no use Jessie protesting. Lavinia, this time with her fingers in her ears, had dived back into her book.

'Background!' said Jessica, crossly.

21

Fractions

ONE AFTERNOON LAVINIA FORGOT TO
come home from her music lesson. She disappeared at
four o'clock and didn't come back for ages.

This caused great agitation at the Select Seminary.
Miss Minchin fumed, and Miss Amelia twittered and
chewed her finger ends. Cook said, 'Well, it wouldn't be
the first time one of the young madams has taken herself
off next door and never come back.'

This untactful remark sent Miss Minchin into an even
worse temper. Cook was ordered to hold her tongue.
Miss Amelia was told she should remember her age and
try to assume a little dignity, the entire schoolroom (who
overheard this conversation and were detected giggling)

were given an indigestible chunk of Bible to learn, and Alice was sent to recapture Lavinia.

Alice didn't come back for ages either.

'Gossiping with the kitchen staff!' guessed Miss Minchin acidly (and accurately). 'Well, there is no shortage of scullery maids in London, Amelia. You may tell Alice, when she chooses to return, that if such a thing happens again she will be immediately dismissed!'

'Yes, Maria,' agreed Miss Amelia, with no intention of doing any such thing. Alice had only arrived at the Select Seminary a few weeks before, and yet already Miss Amelia could not imagine how they had managed without her. She really was a treasure. Only the day before she had performed the superhuman feat of washing the hair of the entire little ones' dormitory. All eight had been vigorously scrubbed with liquid green soap, rinsed with rosemary water (as in Epping), rubbed, combed and braided. This dreadful job, and the shrieks, wrigglings, splashings and tears that went with it, had previously been Miss Amelia's fate. Never, never, never, thought Miss Amelia, would she do or say anything that would send her rescuer heading back to Epping.

'As for Lavinia,' continued Miss Minchin, 'I shall

speak to her myself. In the parlour. Kindly send her to me the moment she arrives.'

Lavinia did not have a nice time in the parlour with Miss Minchin.

'She says if I am ever so late again she will stop me going,' she reported when she rejoined the girls in the schoolroom. 'I do think another time if it seems that I am going to be late one of you might bang on the wall. I would hear that. It's just on the other side of where we are working.'

'Is it? We never hear a piano.'

'Well, obviously they are quite thick walls,' said Lavinia irritably. 'I don't see why you shouldn't. It isn't much to ask you to do.'

'I don't mind trying,' offered Ermengarde, but Jessica, who was tired of Lavinia's perpetual music lessons, said, 'If the walls are so thick we don't hear your piano playing, how do you suppose you would notice our banging?'

'Anyway, what would Miss Amelia and Miss Minchin say if they caught us hammering on the walls?' added Gertrude.

'You're not very helpful,' snapped Lavinia crossly. 'I

suppose I shall have to rely on Ermengarde, then. I can't
see that being much use! Ermengarde, *why* do you chew
your ribbon like that!'

'It helps me think.'

'It doesn't seem to help *much*,' commented Lavinia,
looking with disgust at Ermengarde's blotted pages.
'Why is your work all crossed out?'

'Because it's all wrong.'

'But they are only fractions,' said Lavinia. 'They are
as easy as anything! Jessie can do them, for goodness'
sake! *Gertrude* can do them! Look at that first one!
Nothing could be more simple. Draw a cake . . .'

'I don't really like cake,' said Ermengarde.

'Oh, how silly! An orange then! Draw an orange! Now
divide it into eight slices. Look at your orange, and look
at your sum! You are adding quarters and eighths. A
quarter is two eighths. A half is four eighths. Put all your
fractions into eighths, and add them up. Go on! Write
down the answer!'

'But is that it?' asked Ermengarde.

'Yes, of course. Now look at the next one. It's in
quarters and thirds. You will need to make everything
into twelfths.'

'I've never even heard of twelfths!' moaned Ermengarde.

'Of course you have! Think! Suppose you had your shilling pocket money, and you had to give a third of it for a new ribbon (you wouldn't get a very nice ribbon for that much but I suppose it would be good enough to chew) and a quarter of it to church collection (I don't think it's fair that we have to give so much when the little ones get away with a penny). How would you do it? You can't chop up a shilling.'

'I would change it for pennies,' said Ermengarde at last. 'Twelve pennies. Four for the ribbon, three for church . . .'

'Well, then you have heard of twelfths! Pennies are twelfths!'

'But you can't change an orange into pennies!'

'No, but you can change it into twelfths.'

'But it's already in eights!' protested Ermengarde.

'A *new* orange!' said Lavinia. 'They are imaginary oranges, you can have as many as you like! Draw it! That's right! Now look at your sum. From three quarters take one third. How many twelfths is three quarters? Nine! And one third? Four!

Take four from nine!'

'Five,' said Ermengarde. 'Five slices of orange. Five twelfths. Is that the answer?'

'Yes.'

'But it's quite easy!' wailed Ermengarde, aghast at the discovery that the thing which had caused her so much anguish was so very simple.

'They are all easy! I told you that! Now the next is in thirds and sevenths. Draw,' ordered Lavinia, suddenly enjoying herself very much, 'a bunch of twenty-one grapes . . .'

Ermengarde had offered to try and save Lavinia from being late a second time. Lavinia, in return, with a combination of airy efficiency and invisible fruit, taught Ermengarde how to add and subtract fractions. She did it so well that Ermengarde managed a whole page of sums from top to bottom without a single mistake.

'Although it does feel like cheating to use so many oranges and grapes and things,' she said worriedly to Jessica when Lavinia had whisked out of the room to study economics in peace upstairs. 'Do you think it's all right?'

'I use strings of beads,' said Jessica. 'Lavinia showed me how, ages ago. She's a very good teacher. I expect it will be all right.'

22

I Know All Your Names

ERMENGARDE WAS ALL RIGHT, OR AT least her fractions were, and she was so grateful that the next time it seemed that Lavinia had forgotten to reappear from her music lesson she put on the blue cloak and slipped out of the house to remind her.

'Ah ha!' said the red-headed boy, throwing open the door as suddenly as if he had been watching out for her. 'I know what you are here for! You've come to tell Lav it's chucking out time!'

'Well, I . . .'

'You're Ermengarde. I know all your names.'

'Oh . . .'

'And the secrets of the Pudding Shop, you'll be astonished to hear, are secrets no longer! We've heard every detail, from the basement to the attic! Something very nasty up there, she says!'

'Who says? Not Lavin—'

'No, of course not! No gossip from old Lav! Far too busy swotting! Now then, is it rats, or is it ghosts? I know which I prefer! Don't just hover on the doorstep like that. Come in!'

'Thank you but . . .'

'So aren't you lucky, you Pudding-Shoppers, living in a haunted house!'

'I'm sure . . .'

'Well yes, you're absolutely right! If the Pudding Shop has ghosts, then this house should, too. They walk through walls, don't they? Superb! I shall start ghost-watching. Guess how I learned your names?'

'I really don't . . .'

'Dragged 'em out of old Lav! Like this, listen!'

There was a half-open door in the passage behind the red-headed boy. He turned and yelled towards it, 'Black-haired stumpy one?'

'Oh shut up, Tristram,' came Lavinia's voice.

'Come on! You must know! Wears a red hat on Sundays.'

'Gertrude,' snapped Lavinia.

'See?' said the boy to Ermengarde, 'I've got her trained to reply!' and raising his voice again he called, 'Curly Bosco burglar? Can't behave in church.'

'Lottie. You know that one perfectly well.'

'Big square face and never stops talking! Threw a duster at me!'

'That's Alice. She's just a maid.'

'Grins whenever I look at her and thinks she's very pretty.'

'Jessie *is* pretty,' said Lavinia, coming into the hall laden with books. 'Ermengarde! What are you doing here?'

'She came to remind you not to stay all night. Right then, here's another one for you. Terrible old dragon. Drunk as a lord!'

'I must hurry,' said Lavinia coldly. 'Please thank your uncle for me and tell him I will see him tomorrow. Ermengarde, it was nice of you to come. Did Miss Minchin say you might?'

'Goodness no! She never would! But she doesn't

notice me when I wear this cloak.'

'She will notice you if we both go back together, though. I think I had better go in first, and you can follow a minute or two afterwards. I will get Miss Minchin away from the front door somehow or other.'

Getting Miss Minchin away from the door was easy. She was waiting for Lavinia, and the moment she arrived she hurried her into the parlour, exclaiming with great agitation, 'Lavinia, I should like a private word!'

'Miss Minchin?'

'That girl!' said Miss Minchin accusingly, pacing the room between door and windows. 'Does she visit next door? Does she?'

Ermengarde, thought Lavinia, and her heart sank at the thought of the fuss Miss Minchin would make if she had seen Ermengarde creeping round to remind her of the time. All the same she replied, very quickly and brightly, 'Which girl, Miss Minchin? Quite a number of people visit there, students, or pupils for music lessons. And Tristram's sisters . . .'

But Miss Minchin was hardly listening.

'I believe she has some plan to ruin me! I *know* she is

still close by! Over and over I glimpse her . . .'

She *can't* mean Ermengarde, thought Lavinia. What *is* she talking about?

'. . . Always in that cloak . . .'

'A *cloak*, Miss Minchin?' asked Lavinia. 'One of us?'

Lavinia's voice implied that cloaks were not at all the sort of things that young ladies at a Select Seminary would choose to wear.

'I am not talking of our girls!' snapped Miss Minchin, but before she could say more she was interrupted by the arrival of Miss Amelia.

'It is time for Lavinia to come to supper,' said Miss Amelia, shooing Lavinia out of the door as she spoke. 'Hurry and wash your hands, dear, quickly please! Off you go!'

Miss Minchin seemed to collapse, slumping at her table with her fingers to her temples.

'And it is time you stopped this dreadful worrying, Maria,' continued Miss Amelia, bravely confronting her sister. 'Nobody has plans to ruin you! Nobody creeps through the house at night! Nobody understands what you are talking about, dear!'

'*I know* nobody understands what I am talking about!'

wailed Miss Minchin, and as she spoke she had a sudden clear memory of standing in that same room, aged eight or nine years old, bleating, over and over, the very same self-pitying words.

('She will make herself ill,' her mother had said, gazing helplessly at her unlovable little daughter, while Maria's father had disgustedly ordered, 'Send in the girl to settle her!' and made haste to hurry out of the room.)

Miss Amelia was a kinder person than either of her parents had been, but even so, not much had changed.

'Maria,' she said gently, 'you will make yourself ill.' And as she moved towards the parlour door she added, 'I will send in Alice to settle you . . .'

And then she, too, had hurried out of the room.

Ermengarde did manage to return to the Select Seminary unobserved, but all evening she was rather thoughtful. She was pondering the awful and accurate descriptions of people that the red-headed boy shouted at Lavinia. She couldn't help wondering what her own had been.

So in the end I asked Lavinia! she wrote to Sara. *And when she told me I was so astonished.*

I couldn't believe it.

I said, 'Are you sure you didn't mishear?'

'Yes, quite,' said Lavinia, in her iciest voice. (She really doesn't like anyone suggesting she might have made a mistake.)

'And you knew it was me that he meant?'

'Ermengarde, I really am very busy,' said Lavinia. 'And I can't understand why you are so surprised. You heard what he said about the others!'

That's why I am so surprised.

Ermengarde paused, remembering that astonishing conversation with Lavinia. She had begged, 'Tell me what he said one more time and then I promise I'll go away.'

'He said,' (Lavinia had repeated, in a pretend-patient voice) '"Lav!" (I hate him calling me that!) "Who's the goldy one?"'

Ermengarde wrote it down.

The goldy one.

On paper the words looked even more unbelievable. Ermengarde had led an unappreciated life. No one, not even Sara, had ever suggested that the round, worried face that she saw in the mirror every morning might ever look anything else but round and worried. She had grown up knowing she was dull and plain and uninteresting.

Ermengarde read the words again, and then carefully she folded the paper, and very gently tore along the crease she had made.

The goldy one, read the slip of paper.

Ermengarde fell asleep with it still in her hand, and all night she held it very tightly, like a sort of fragile magic that might vanish in the morning.

23

The Reason that Bosco Dribbled in His Sleep

BOSCO SLEPT ON THE OLD WING CHAIR IN the corner of the kitchen. From time to time he snored a little, and licked his lips. He dreamed, with longing, of the Select Seminary.

For years and years, ever since he could remember, Bosco had dined on fish heads on weekdays and liver on Sundays. On weekday nights he had dreamed of liver, and on Sunday nights he had dreamed of fish heads, and he had been perfectly content.

But since Bosco's discovery of the Select Seminary those days were gone.

He had learned of other, more delicious foods.

Macaroni cheese, and boiled cod. Lumps of sausage and shoe-flavoured milk. Deliciously sulphury scrambled eggs. Ham that shone with a greenish metal light and mutton by the fistful. Strange things called rissoles with fishy insides. The mysterious, gluey middles of pies.

No wonder Bosco dribbled in his sleep.

24

Five Minutes Late (as Usual)

ERMENGARDE HAD A PARCEL. IT ARRIVED by carrier very early one morning and was handed to Lottie, who happened to be alone on the doorstep at the time, sploshing about with a scrubbing brush.

'I shall need it signed for,' said the driver, so Lottie obligingly signed with the stump of pencil that he produced from behind one of his ears. Then she carried it upstairs and dumped it on Ermengarde's chest while she was still asleep.

'Get off, get off!' groaned Ermengarde.

'It's morning and you've got a parcel,' announced Lottie. 'I signed for it all by myself while Alice was doing the boots! I've been awake for hours. I've sifted the parlour ashes, too! I bet you don't know how to do that!'

'I don't know what Miss Minchin would say if she knew you'd been signing for parcels and sifting ashes,' commented Ermengarde, sitting up and rubbing her sleepy eyes.

'She'd tear up the turf,' said Lottie cheerfully. 'That's what Alice says. It means she'd go wild and furious, like a mad bull. Do hurry up, Ermie, and open it. Perhaps it's another great big cake from your Aunt Eliza.'

'I've had enough cakes from Aunt Eliza,' said Ermengarde ungratefully, tugging at the wrappings. 'Anyway, I don't suppose she'll send me anything ever again, now she has my horrible tablecloth . . . Oh! It's from Sara . . .'

'What has she sent? What has she sent?'

'I don't know. I hope not more shells, the last ones got a bit smelly. Here's a letter too.'

'Would you like me to unpack the parcel, while you read the letter?' asked Lottie helpfully.

'If you like.'

It was a long letter, thanking Ermengarde for the funny postcard, remembering Lottie, describing Sara's walks through the little seaside town where she was staying. Ermengarde read it aloud.

It is so quiet here, wrote Sara. *When we first came Becky thought it was much too quiet. 'It's like when there is straw down in the street,' she said. She was thinking of the time when they put straw down in the square, do you remember, Ermie? When the old gentleman at the corner was so ill, and they wanted to lessen the noise of horses and wheels in the road. And we all had to walk to church the long way round past the vicarage and Miss Minchin said it was most inconvenient and she hoped he would not linger. Becky said it felt like someone was lingering here!*

She is more used to it now, and she has made great friends with the boy in the sweet shop. The sweet shop is a storybook place, Ermie, with a little bow window almost as low as the pavement, and a door knocker shaped like a dolphin. When you go in you step down on to a mat and that makes a bell ring in the room at the back. Inside the light is quite dim, and the sweets in their glass jars shine like jewels. I wish Lottie could see it. Even more I wish that you were here and could walk with me along the sloping cobbled streets that end in a view of sea. That's the way I like to go best, but we don't very often because Becky says the sea has a cold look and gives her the chills. Becky likes much more to go into town, especially to the sweet shop, and so does Boris. You remember Boris, Ermengarde? The big dog that Uncle Tom bought for me for a surprise. I am afraid he is getting rather fat. It is partly sweets, and partly that he does not get enough exercise. It is hard to keep a boar hound healthy. Unluckily, Ram Dass does not like dogs. (Many Indian people are the same.) So although he takes care of the monkey (do you remember the little monkey who climbed into my attic over the roof from next door?) he does not like to do anything for Boris. And Boris is very naughty. He ran away on the beach and lost his gold and silver collar, I cannot imagine how. (But I am a little glad because it was rather embarrassing. People would read it, and then I would have to try to explain without hurting Uncle Tom's feelings that it was only a joke, and that I was not a princess, and that I would never have chosen those words, even if I was.) So anyway, as I was telling you, Becky and I have to exercise Boris and since Becky does not like the beach that means we usually walk into the town, and often to the sweet shop. The sweet-shop boy gives toffees to Boris and that is why he is getting rather fat.

As you can see, Becky and I visited it today and bought enough sweets for the whole school! I hope they enjoy them, and I hope you like this purple ribbon I am sending, Ermie. It is just the colour of my new dress. There is a little kaleidoscope in the parcel too, for Lottie.

We will not be staying here much longer, Ermengarde. Uncle Tom and I have been making such plans! But I had better not say any more because Becky does not know yet and I am not sure how pleased she will be. I don't think Becky likes adventures. Yesterday I asked her what she would like to do most in the world and she said she would like to show Arthur round the square (Arthur is the sweet-shop boy). 'And walk him past the Select Seminary,' she said. 'I've told him all about it. Them lovely tiles in the hall, and the coloured glass in the door, and the young ladies and the dinners that was cooked. I hope the new girl is keeping that brass plate properly clean!'

'Goodness, Becky!' I said, laughing rather. 'Why ever should you care?'

'I used to keep it lovely,' said Becky. 'Nobody, not even Miss Minchin, could fault the way I kept that brass plate!'

'Poor Becky!' commented Lottie. 'It's a good job she can't see it now. It is all green in the corners from being done with spit. Alice says she cannot abide the smell of brass polish and neither can I! What else does Sara say?'

I think about you all very often, because, of course, I know exactly what you are doing every moment of the day. I think, now they are having their supper, or walking twice round the square, or learning their Sunday Bible verses. The other morning, at five minutes past eight, I couldn't help laughing because I suddenly thought, Now Ermengarde is five minutes late for prayers! (Because you know you nearly always are, Ermie!)

This parcel will arrive on Saturday, and this evening you will all be folding your weekday petticoats for the Monday laundry, and shaking out your Sunday ones to be ready for church tomorrow! It is such fun to know those things when I am not there!

'Oh really!' growled Ermengarde. 'She need not gloat so much! It's all very well for her! Look at the time, Lottie! We *will* be late for prayers!'

'Not me,' said Lottie cheerfully. 'I'm dressed.'

'Sunday petticoats!' grumbled Ermengarde, bundling Sara's letter under her pillow. 'Why did she have to remind me? I'd forgotten all about the horrid thing! I put my foot through the lace last week and now it is dangling all round the hem. I suppose I shall have to try and sew it up! Find my stockings, Lottie, do! And your pinafore is inside out and your hands are ashy! Will my hair do if I just comb the front?'

'I don't think so,' said Lottie, dabbing her grey hands on Ermengarde's sponge, tying her unbrushed curls with a fragment of tape and miraculously producing a clean pinafore by twisting the ashy one right side round. 'I've found your stockings though, if you don't mind one being black and one being grey! I'm going now, I'm all ready!'

She skipped out of the room, just as the bell rang for morning prayers. A little while later Ermengarde followed, odd-stockinged, messy-haired, grumpy and flustered, five minutes late as usual.

25

Becky

MILES AWAY, IN THE LITTLE SEASIDE
town, Sara was crying, and it was Becky's fault.

'Oh!' cried Becky woefully. 'Oh, don't take on, Miss
Sara, please! I'll tell Arthur no, and stay with you always.
We'll have adventures, just like you said. After all, I
promised you first.'

'No, no, of course you didn't!'

'We'll go back to India! That'd be an adventure,
wouldn't it, Miss Sara? On a ship, like when you come
here all that time ago.'

'Darling Becky,' said Sara, in a rather wobbly voice.

Being called a darling lifted Becky's spirits
tremendously. 'Over the sea and everything!' she

continued bravely. 'It can't be as deep as it looks! They'd never get the fish out if it was . . .'

'Oh, I do love you, Becky!'

'And we'll ride on elephants like your papa used to do, and visit them diamond mines and check you're getting fair play from your Uncle Tom . . .'

'Becky!'

'You has to think of these things, miss! It's not as if he's real family, is it? You need taking care of, Miss Sara. I should never have thought of nothing else! Only Arthur . . .'

'Becky,' interrupted Sara, turning to reach out to Becky's suddenly trembling shoulder and giving it a friendly little shake. 'Listen to me! You should do exactly what makes you most happy and not worry for a moment about anybody else.'

'Oh no I shouldn't, miss,' said Becky at once. 'Whatever would the world be like if everyone did that? And where'd I be, if it wasn't for you? Down in the kitchen at Miss Minchin's, most like. Being shouted at by Cook!'

Sara gave a little smile.

'Oooh, she did have a temper,' continued Becky. 'Do

you recall the time she threw the clock at the butcher, Miss Sara? And you and me in the scullery dying with laughter! *What* a temper! And then the next minute as cheerful as you please, and she'd put a teacosy on her head and take off Miss Amelia saying her prayers in church! And the pies she made! I've told Arthur about those pies! I've told Arthur about all of it.'

'Becky . . .'

'Now, never you worry about Arthur,' said Becky. 'He'll not be lonely long, a fine-looking lad like him and that little shop to do as he likes with. Twenty-one next birthday and as nice a nature as a millionaire . . . I daresay you noticed, miss?'

'Yes, of course I did, Becky.'

'Twenty-one, and me coming up at eighteen, seemed suitable, you see.'

'Becky!' said Sara, suddenly very stern. 'You must forget about me and marry Arthur at once! You silly, kind, faithful Becky! How could you have thought of doing anything else?'

This speech had a most dramatic effect upon Becky. She flung her apron over her head and collapsed on to the nearest seat, where she rocked backwards and forwards.

'Becky, whatever is the matter now?' Sara cried.

'Oh, miss,' exclaimed Becky, emerging from her apron at last. 'I'm that grateful, miss, I never could say! And I'm that happy! And we'll call our first little girl after you, Miss Sara, because I never could forget about you, never, never, never!'

And then there was a good deal of crying and hugging, and soon Becky rubbed her eyes and laughed and asked, 'What'll they say at the Select Seminary when they hear I'm to be married? Will Miss Amelia be jealous, poor thing? Do you suppose Cook will make us a cake?'

'Becky, you *should* be happy!' Sara exclaimed. 'You *deserve* to be happy! Just listen to you! All those dreadful times you had there, and yet you can still think of them and laugh!'

'You will as well, one day, miss,' said Becky, tenderly. 'I'm older than you, Miss Sara, I've had time to learn things you haven't yet. And one of them is, that dreadful times passes. And you laughs about them after, miss.

'You wait and see,' promised Becky.

26

Something Behind All This

ERMENGARDE CARRIED HER PARCEL DOWN
to the schoolroom after morning lessons were finished.
Sugared almonds, chocolate caramels and lemon drops
were passed around and Jessie tied the new purple ribbon
into a large flapping bow on Ermengarde's plait.

'It looks like a chocolate box ribbon,' commented
Lottie, peering at it through her kaleidoscope. The
kaleidoscope showed multiple images of everything it
was directed at: dozens of girls, an impossible number
of lemon drops, the schoolroom fire a tangle of flames.

'Thank you,' wrote the school on a postcard supplied
by Ermengarde (*The Thames at High Tide*), and signed

their names with little messages.

'A tooth came out in my caramel, Lottie X'

'Do you have any diamonds yet?
Your old friend, Gertrude'

'It is a nice purple, much nicer than purple
usually is, from Ermengarde'

'Lavinia would write but she is so busy, love Jessie'

Miss Minchin had never objected to her pupils receiving parcels. They arrived quite often at the Select Seminary, heavy packages of books despatched by Ermengarde's ever hopeful father, trinkets from France from Lavinia's mother, dreadful knitted vests and home made liberty bodices for Jessica, constructed by her grandmother, who had, said Jessica ungratefully, far too little to do. Miss Minchin smiled gracefully on all these tokens of affection, if their receivers did not. Not only did they raise morale but also they substantially reduced the housekeeping bills. The list of Useful and Acceptable Gifts to Pupils (helpfully sent to parents at the beginning of each school year) was very long indeed, and as well as cakes, biscuits, books and clothes, it included such surprises as cheese and paper, ink and soap.

Once Miss Amelia bravely remarked that it looked far too much like a grocery order.

'Nonsense!' said Miss Minchin, adding tooth powder and candles.

In the past, the only times that Miss Minchin had ever complained about the parcels her pupils received was when she was not informed of their arrival, and consequently had no time to adjust the menus for the day. However, since the winter morning when the ragged Sara had received her parcels of lovely clothes, and Miss Minchin's world had come tumbling down, things had changed at the Select Seminary. Now Miss Minchin demanded that not only was she informed of the arrival of every parcel, but also that they were unpacked in her presence.

'No more underhand goings on in *this* house!' she had ordered. 'See that you are vigilant, Amelia!'

Today it seemed that Amelia had not been vigilant after all.

'Why,' demanded Miss Minchin, as the girls were filing past her to take their afternoon walk (twice round the square) 'are the young ladies all sucking sweets? How did this occur?'

'I believe one of them had a parcel, dear,' said Miss Amelia. 'I assumed you had said they might open it. Did you not?'

'I certainly did not! And, what is more, I was in the hall when the post arrived this morning. There was nothing but letters. Of that I am quite sure! Ermengarde St John, is that a new ribbon you are wearing? Where did it come from?'

Ermengarde hesitated. It was always an ordeal, mentioning Sara's name to Miss Minchin. 'I f-f-found it in a parcel, Miss Minchin,' she stammered at last.

'A parcel?'

'Yes, Miss Minchin.'

'You have had a parcel recently?'

'Yes. Today, Miss Minchin.'

'There were no parcels delivered today,' stated Miss Minchin flatly.

'Oh, but it came . . .' Ermengarde began and then paused again. 'Earlier by carrier,' she had started to say, before she noticed that Lottie was standing behind Miss Minchin and making the most tremendous shushing signals. Of course, realised Ermengarde, she must not say it had arrived by carrier, not when Lottie had been the person to sign for it.

'Yes?' prompted Miss Minchin. 'It came . . . ?'

'I am not quite sure when it came,' murmured Ermengarde confusedly. 'It . . . it just arrived in my bedroom. Somehow, I suppose.'

Lottie rushed to the rescue.

'I helped unwrap it, Miss Minchin!' she volunteered, bouncing up in front of Ermengarde and pushing her surreptitiously towards the open front door as she spoke. 'There was a little kaleidoscope thing in it for me. And all sorts of sweets, lemon drops and caramels and almonds. And Ermie's ribbon, of course. It's a funny purple, but she likes it, don't you, Ermengarde? Oh, she's gone with Miss Amelia! . . . Miss Minchin, must I go for a walk today? I am so tired and one of my legs feels funny. I'll show you!'

Then, before Miss Minchin could fully grasp Lottie's intentions, the youngest pupil of the Select Seminary began hauling up the complex layers of wool and flounced muslin and feather-stitched flannel that concealed her black-stockinged legs. Nor did she stop when the appalled Miss Minchin exploded: 'Lottie Legh!

What do you think you are doing?'

'I'm showing you my funny knee. I think I might have caught rheumatics from poor old Cook. There is a sort of knobbly bit . . .'

'Lottie!'

'. . . here you see, at the top . . .'

'Lottie, stop this disgracefully unladylike exhibition immediately!' thundered Miss Minchin. 'Pull up your stocking at once! To think that I should ever see one of my pupils unhooking her suspenders in the middle in the front hall!'

'Just let me show you the other knee and then you can compare,' begged Lottie, unhooking even more, but Miss Minchin had enough.

'Out you go *immediately*!' she ordered. 'No, *not like that! Respectably* dressed, you disgraceful child! Why are you sitting on the floor?'

'I always do my suspenders on the floor,' said Lottie comfortably. 'Else I fall over.'

'Stand up! Pull down your petticoats! And the back of your dress! Now go at once, and apologise to Miss Amelia for your lateness.'

Lottie skipped down the steps and into the street

congratulating herself on having managed to distract Miss Minchin so cunningly. Inside the house Miss Minchin leaned her forehead against the green-painted hall wall and closed her eyes for a few moments. Then she pulled herself together, descended the basement stairs and demanded to know who had signed for the parcel that Miss Ermengarde received that morning. She looked particularly hard at Alice as she asked, but Alice, who had been inside cleaning boots when the carrier arrived, told Miss Minchin perfectly truthfully that she knew nothing about it.

'Likely it didn't come by post at all,' suggested Cook. 'Someone local handed it over, a friend maybe, on the quiet.'

'How could that happen?' demanded Miss Minchin.

'Girls, even young ladies, even *our* young ladies, can be sly,' said Cook. 'Look at that Miss Diamond Mines! She was a sly puss if I ever knew one! Madam! Madam, are you not well?'

For Miss Minchin was suddenly quite pale.

'Sara Crewe!' she said. 'I should have guessed . . . I should have guessed . . .'

'Madam, you should sit down a minute!' interrupted

Cook, quite alarmed. 'Bless my soul, she's all a tremble! Alice, a glass of water! Hurry, girl!'

'She's here!' said Miss Minchin hoarsely.

'Yes, madam, here she is, with a glass of water. Take a sip now.'

'Not Alice!' said Miss Minchin, pushing the glass away. 'Sara! Sara Crewe!'

'No, madam,' said Cook as soothingly as she could. 'On the south coast she is, madam, with that Indian gentleman. Letters come, now and then. I've seen the postmark.'

Miss Minchin, with her fingers once more to her temples, almost moaned.

'She is *haunting* me!' she exclaimed.

Behind Miss Minchin's head Cook rolled her eyes to the ceiling. Out loud she said, 'Haunting you! What a thing to say! She is far from dead! She's as alive as you and I, madam, and so is that useless hussy Becky as went with her.'

'Miss Ermengarde,' said Miss Minchin, seizing Cook's arm and holding it very tightly, 'said she found the parcel in her room, Cook! Explain that!'

'Her carafe from the parlour, quick!' mouthed Cook

to Alice, over Miss Minchin's head.

Alice disappeared.

'Miss Ermengarde,' said Cook, detaching her arm from Miss Minchin's grasp as she spoke, 'doesn't know what day of the week it is half the time! She wanders round with that ribbon in her mouth and dressed like I don't know what (odd stockings this morning, I noticed!). *Hardly* to be relied on, that one, if you ask me. Now, here's Alice, madam, with your . . . with your special medicinal . . . your herbal . . . (that's right, pour her a stiff one, Alice!). There you are, madam!'

'It is a nerve tonic, Cook,' said Miss Minchin, swallowing with her eyes closed.

'I'm glad to hear it,' said Cook. 'Alice, take it back up upstairs again now before . . . '

'. . . she wants another!' she mouthed at Alice's raised eyebrows. 'Shall you be all right now, madam?'

'I shall find out what is going on,' said Miss Minchin, getting unsteadily to her feet. 'There is something behind all this! I have suspected for some time . . . I have heard things at night. I have seen a figure in that blue cloak . . . '

'Seeing things, now!' Cook hissed Alice, who had just reappeared.

'My sister says it is all imagination . . .'

'Very likely, madam,' said Cook, not very sympathetically. 'Alice, help your mistress up the stairs, and then go and tell Miss Amelia she is not herself . . .'

'I am completely myself!' said Miss Minchin, with dignity. 'I will take a little rest in my parlour before my afternoon duties begin. Thank you for your help, Cook. Alice, your hair is a disgrace.'

'It's flying up and down these stairs that does it,' said Alice, cheerfully, leading her out of the door. 'I shall just take your arm, miss, so we don't have no staggering, that's right . . . and into the parlour (mind the mat) and on to the sofa you go, and shut your eyes and no one but me and Cook any the wiser . . .'

'And I hadn't the door shut, ' related Alice to Cook, 'before she was reaching . . .'

'Ahh!' said Cook, ponderously.

'Poor old thing!'

'She's a shocker, if you ask me,' said Cook.

'"Something behind all this!" indeed! What's behind all this is as clear as water and five and six a bottle!'

'I still say she's a poor old thing,' said Alice.

27

Aunt Eliza

ERMENGARDE'S AUNT ELIZA HAD ALWAYS been considered the family fool, first by her brother, Ermengarde's father, and then by her husband.

'And they were right,' admitted Aunt Eliza. 'I was. What could be more foolish than to allow myself to be made miserable for a lifetime . . . *a lifetime!* . . . by two silly men! Two silly *bald* men! Two silly, *bald*, narrow-minded, impractical, selfish . . .'

'I musn't be bitter,' said Aunt Eliza when her husband died. 'To be bitter would be still to be miserable. I am free now. I can do as I like.'

The problem for Aunt Eliza was that, although she

knew very clearly what she didn't like (having done it for a lifetime), she did not know what she liked. She had to discover it.

One of the first things Aunt Eliza discovered she liked doing was sending cakes to Ermengarde. Beautiful cakes. Even after they were dispatched she liked to think of them, recalling in detail their shapes and recipes, the prettiness of their icing, the neatness of their packaging. In her mind Aunt Eliza packed and repacked the cherry cake hamper, tied and retied the pink bows on the white birthday box. It made her very happy, and she imagined that it made Ermengarde very happy too.

Aunt Eliza would probably have gone on for years and years, sending cakes to Ermengarde, if one day she had not happened to receive a parcel herself.

It was Ermengarde's horrible tablecloth.

The first thing Aunt Eliza did after she had unpacked the tablecloth was hurry upstairs and into a room that was never used. The room contained a heavy dark chest. From the bottom drawer, a drawer that smelled of old wood and dust and ancient air, she lifted a piece of fabric. A sampler made by herself at Ermengarde's age.

Aunt Eliza took it downstairs with her, and in the

clean air of her sitting room she laid the tablecloth and the sampler side by side. Even after so many years she found it hard to look steadily at the sampler, but she inspected the tablecloth very carefully, stooping over it with the magnifying glass she kept on her desk, feeling with her fingertips the puckered hem and the grey knotted threads, following with care the trails of tiny rust-coloured dots that shadowed every stitch.

'Good heavens!' said Aunt Eliza.

She was very much disturbed.

28

Two Letters

'THERE ARE TWO LETTERS FOR YOU ON the hall table!' Gertrude rushed to tell Ermengarde one morning. 'Miss Amelia has just put out the post.'

It was surprising the excitement that the arrival of the post caused at the Select Seminary, considering the uselessness of most of the Young Ladies' relations. Miss Minchin's long-ago plan to attract parents who were detached, abroad, uninterested or dead had succeeded magnificently. Very few of her pupils were given any encouragement by their families to think that they would ever be of much importance to them again. Yet it was expected that some sort of communication should be kept up between home and Seminary. Consequently, letters arrived every day. They were received by their owners with the highest of hopes, despite long experience having taught them that they might contain any number of horrors. Gertrude's French godmother persisted in her unreasonable demands for French replies. Jessica's grandmamma asked impertinent questions concerning the thickness and extent of her granddaughter's underwear. Lavinia's mother sent a perpetual supply of very good reasons not to have her daughter home for the holidays, and Ermengarde's father regularly included Latin quotations. And yet, every morning the envelopes were seized and ripped open with eager hands. A small silence would follow, while the readers scanned the pages for news of the outside world, and then the schoolroom would fill with murmurs of dismay, indignant comments and occasional unladylike but honest opinions.

Ermengarde's two letters came from Sara and her Aunt Eliza. She opened them both at once, and read them in alternate chunks, turning from one to the other. All around her there were mutters and shrieks, as other people read their own letters.

'Not a single word about rabbits *again*!'

'*Yellow ribbons!* Mother is far too old for any sort of ribbons!'

'Hurray, Great-uncle George is dead at last! . . . He had such nasty, meaty hands . . . No, I'm not being horrid, he'll be in Heaven, won't he?'

'Mamma is having new paper hung in my room, pink and silver stripes,' said Jessica contentedly. Jessica had always been loved.

Ermengarde's Aunt Eliza had never learned the art of breaking bad news. Her letter to Ermengarde plunged straight into her concerns, with no softening good wishes, thanks for tablecloths, or references to cake.

> *My Very Dearest Ermengarde,*
> *Reluctant as I am to suggest anything that might cause distress . . .*

That typical Aunt Eliza beginning caused Ermengarde to drop her letter very quickly and pick up Sara's instead.

> *Ermie, such an exciting thing is going to happen . . .*

If there was one thing, thought Ermengarde, who was in a particularly grumpy mood that morning, worse than being trapped in the Select Seminary like a bird in a cage, it was being trapped there while your previous fellow captive wrote heartless gloating letters about the world beyond the bars.

Ermengarde growled, put down Sara, and picked up Aunt Eliza instead.

My dear, I knew what your problem was the moment I opened your parcel.

My tablecloth, groaned Ermengarde. She's got it! This is going to be a terrible letter! What was Sara saying? *More* diamonds, I suppose . . . Oh, no, it's about Becky. She's saving the diamonds till later.

Darling Becky . . . she likes her better than me, thought Ermengarde . . . *is to be married. She is so happy that I am trying to be pleased for her, although when I first heard the news I was dreadfully upset. He is called Arthur, Arthur from the sweet shop. (I wrote to you about him only last week.) He is tallish, with rather awful red hair . . .*

I *like* red hair! thought Ermengarde indignantly. The boy next door has red hair!

. . . but he has a nice smile and is very polite. Uncle Tom

says he is a blessing as he was wondering what to do about Becky, and I suppose I am getting used to the idea. We invited him to tea yesterday, so that we could get to know him a little better. It was rather difficult to talk, though. He doesn't seem to care at all for books . . .

Sara cares too much about books! thought Ermengarde irritably. She always did. She is as bad as Lavinia in her way.

Ermengarde put down Sara's letter, and picked up Aunt Eliza's again. At least Aunt Eliza wasn't intelligent. That was one good thing about her!

Aunt Eliza was evidently feeling guilty.

Now that I am free, she had written (*I am sure you understand what I mean by that, Ermengarde, and will not think I am criticising poor dear Uncle Julius in anyway*) *I would like to see a great deal more of you . . .*

'Why are you looking so surprised, Ermie?' enquired Lottie.

'Aunt Eliza wants to see a great deal more of me, she says. Lottie, for goodness' sake! Whatever is the matter with you?'

For Lottie was suddenly rolling around the floor squealing with laughter.

'*How* much more?' she demanded, between bursts of giggles.

'I don't know.'

'A great deal sounds an awful lot! Perhaps you will have to be nearly bare!'

'Oh, Lottie, stop it!'

'Get up, you silly vulgar child!' ordered Lavinia, giving Lottie a very sharp prod with her foot.

'Ermie, she kicked me! Do something!'

'I'm busy,' said Ermengarde and picked up Aunt Eliza's letter again.

I see now that I really have not done my duty by you, Ermengarde. Thank goodness, my dear, that you sent me that poor, sad, DREADFUL cloth!

It wasn't that bad! thought Ermengarde, indignantly. I did my best! I slaved for months! She should see the awful pincushion that Becky made for Sara if she thinks that's bad!

Ermengarde pushed away Aunt Eliza's letter in disgust, and picked up Sara's again.

What was Sara saying?

. . . We will be coming up to London to get ready . . .

Why? wondered Ermengarde grumpily. Surely a sweet shop boy could marry a scullery maid without it needing a trip to London.

> *. . . and as soon as I know the exact day I will write and tell you. But it doesn't matter really because I know you are always there . . .*

Always where? wondered Ermengarde.

> *. . . at Miss Minchin's, I mean . . .*
> *. . . I think it may probably be your last chance to say goodbye to Becky . . .*

Becky again. All this fuss about Becky. Ermengarde turned back to Aunt Eliza.

> *I wrote to Miss Minchin and your papa to explain my concerns a few days ago, Ermengarde dear. And with their agreement I have made an appointment to take you to a very fine oculist. I hope the time will be convenient. It is on Saturday next, and afterwards, Ermengarde, to cheer you up (unless you don't care for the idea) Miss Minchin has given me permission to take you out of school. We might eat somewhere nice and then go to the Duke of York's Theatre to see a matinee of the new play (Peter Pan, by Mr J M Barrie. It would be a treat for me too. It is many years since I last went to a theatre). And if you would like to stay with me*

afterwards I am sure we could have a pleasant time together on Sunday . . .

Goodness! thought the astounded Ermengarde. Goodness! Good gracious!

'You look amazed, Ermie,' commented Jessica. 'What is it?'

'Read that!' ordered Ermengarde, pointing to the last paragraph of Aunt Eliza's letter.

'What? Oh yes, I see.'

'I am going to escape for a whole Saturday and Sunday! And go out to lunch! And go to the theatre! Wonderful, wonderful, wonderful Aunt Eliza!'

'If you agree,' said Jessica.

'What?'

Jessica pointed back to the letter.

If you agree, wrote Aunt Eliza.

'*If!*' exclaimed Ermengarde. 'Of course I agree! It's too good to be true!'

'You'd better write and tell her so, then.'

'I shall! I will do it at once! *If* I agree! I'll get my writing case now!'

A few minutes later the message: *Thank you, thank you, Aunt Eliza, thank you I would love it. Thank you, your loving*

Ermengarde had been scribbled on a postcard, stamped with an unnecessary number of stamps and dispatched by way of Alice ('Please take it as soon as you can. It's very urgent!' Ermengarde breathlessly explained).

And then Ermengarde reread her letter from Aunt Eliza and demanded, 'What is an oculist?'

'An oculist,' said Gertrude, 'drills ears.'
  '*Drills ears?*'
  'Yes, it must be frightful,' said Gertrude.

'An oculist,' said Lottie, 'wears turbans. Like in *Arabian Nights*. I thought everyone knew that.'

'An oculist,' said Jessica, 'is something to do with black magic. I know because my cousin had a book called *Tales of the Occult*. My aunt said it was wicked and made her throw it away before she had finished it. But she managed to read enough to see *why* it was wicked. I must say, I'm surprised at *your* aunt, Ermie!'

'I shall ask Lavinia!' said Ermengarde.

29

Don't Be Silly, Ermengarde

'AN OCULIST,' SAID LAVINIA 'IS AN EYE specialist. If you needed to wear spectacles you would go to see an oculist.'

This piece of information sounded so likely to be true that it sent Ermengarde into a turmoil. She read Aunt Eliza's letter again, and realised for the first time the ominous significance of the words, 'to cheer you up'.

Spectacles! she thought bitterly, and at lunchtime she waylaid Alice to demand her postcard back.

'That's long gone,' said Alice, callously dealing out plates of hideous prunes. 'The custard got burned and mind you don't go swallowing prune stones because they grow inside and sprout out through the ears. (There was someone who died of it in Epping.) Now, why are you looking at me like that, Miss Ermengarde? Urgent you said, and urgent it went, and that's that!'

'What's what?' demanded Lottie, but Ermengarde did not reply. All through afternoon lessons she thought of nothing but the horrors of wearing spectacles. Miss Minchin, instructing the Select Seminary on Alfred the Great while simultaneously trying to endure shooting pains in the side of her head, could get no sense from her at all.

'He was an admirably hard-working ruler,' she pronounced. 'In what ways was he so hard-working, Miss St John? Examples, please?'

Ermengarde, who always loathed being called to speak out in class, emerged from her worrying and began to panic.

'I know about his wives,' she said, very flustered. 'But would that count as work? There was Hadrian's Wall. Or was that Hadrian?'

'Continue,' ordered Miss Minchin dangerously.

'The Round Table,' ventured Ermengarde, 'was a very good idea. And probably quite hard work.'

Miss Minchin raised her eyebrows very high.

'Battle of Hastings,' said Ermengarde, losing her head completely, 'and inventing tennis while the Spanish Armada came sailing round the corner. The princes in the tower. And his kingdom for a horse.'

Then to her great relief she was ordered to give up all hope of pudding for a week and sent out of the room in disgrace.

There was no comfort in the bedrooms; Alice had opened the windows that morning to blow away the London germs, and had unfortunately forgotten to close them afterwards. Ermengarde took one look at her freezing, gale-tossed room and headed up to the attic to visit Melchisedec.

Melchisedec was now so tame that he knew Ermengarde's footsteps on the stairs. She would go in to find him standing up, front paws raised, nose twitching, his gaze fixed expectantly on the space where she would appear. He was as stuffed as a cushion. Ermengarde squatted on the floor to stroke him as he gobbled his way through sugar almonds, and a hard-boiled egg that Lottie had refused to eat at breakfast time.

'Lottie said it was old,' she told him apologetically as he ate, 'and it may smell a little of cat. She offered it to Bosco but he only had a lick or two. He'd already had a lot of cod from last night. You must be careful of Bosco. He is here such a lot now . . . Melchisedec . . .'

Melchisedec, who knew his name, looked intelligently up at her.

' . . . Melchisedec, I had a letter from Aunt Eliza. She says I must see an oculist . . .'

Two fat tears rolled down Ermengarde's face.

'I never was pretty,' she said. 'And now spectacles! It isn't fair. I will look like an owl . . .'

Melchisedec was clearly embarrassed. He looked quickly away, and began to stuff huge bites of egg very rapidly, as if he wanted to get the encounter over with as soon as possible.

'Goodness knows what the boy next door will call me when he sees them . . .'

Melchisedec appeared to choke.

'Not that I care,' added Ermengarde. 'Only before . . . Oh, what's the point of talking to you? You're only a rat, after all!'

She had gone too far. She had offended him. He had turned his back on the remains of his egg, and marched away to his hole.

'Come back!' begged Ermengarde. 'I'm sorry! Don't you want an almond? Finish your egg at least! It will dry up and go all horrid . . .'

It was no use. He was gone, and so Ermengarde (feeling rather ashamed) left the attic as well and, finding afternoon lessons were finished, sought out Lavinia for further information. She found her huddled on her bed, wrapped in a quilt, chanting Latin with her eyes on the ceiling.

'Go away,' she ordered, the moment Ermengarde appeared.

'I will in a minute. I just have to ask you, because it's nothing like the others thought. They said turbans and things. So are you absolutely sure, Lavinia?'

'I don't know what on earth you are talking about,' snapped Lavinia, impatiently.

'About an oculist and spectacles.'

'Oh that! Yes of course. Test me on these Latin verbs, please, since you won't go away.'

'I don't know Latin.'

'I know you don't. Just check them in this book as I recite.'

Ermengarde took the book meekly and listened with baffled astonishment as Lavinia recited past, present and future tenses of an unknown language at an impossible speed.

'If you were in Rome,' she asked, when Lavinia at last came to a halt, 'would they understand you?'

'In Ancient Rome they would.'

'Goodness.'

'It's ridiculous to fuss just because you might need to wear spectacles. I shouldn't care a bit if it was me.'

'Yes, but you are pretty. It wouldn't matter so much.'

'Don't be silly, Ermengarde,' said Lavinia.

Was she being silly? wondered Ermengarde, as the days went by. On Friday evening, when Lavinia's definition of an oculist became known in the schoolroom, no one seemed particularly shocked.

'My mamma wears spectacles for reading and sewing,' said Jessica. 'She hangs them on a gold chain. They are pretty. They have little pearl flowers on the sides.'

'I don't suppose Ermengarde's Aunt Eliza will buy her

gold chains and pearl flowers,' commented Gertrude. 'Still, they might make you look a bit more intelligent, Ermengarde. I suppose that can only be good.'

'You're cross because Ermie's going to see *Peter Pan* and you're not,' said Lottie shrewdly.

'I am not! It's nothing but a children's story! I know someone who has seen it and they said it was absolutely silly, all the way through!'

'Oh, Gertrude, no it isn't!' protested Jessie at once. 'It's lovely. I went at Christmas. You should see the stage when it changes to a sea! And the huge ship and the mermaids! And Nana the dog who looks after the children. The children really actually fly, you know! Over the rooftops and through the stars to Neverland . . .'

'Begin at the beginning,' commanded Lottie, and Jessica did, and told the story so well that even Gertrude could not resist staying to listen. And afterwards Jessica described the frock she had worn to visit the theatre, and that led quite naturally to what on earth Ermengarde would wear herself. She and Jessica went upstairs to take out Ermengarde's green and black tartan Sunday frock, and her purple itchy-collared party dress which had something stuck on one of the sleeves and two of the buttons missing.

'You've been wearing that Sunday one ever since I can remember,' said Jessica. 'I can't understand how it still fits.'

'They bought it very big to grow into,' explained Ermengarde, 'and I've got thinner too, since then. But I've grown upwards as well. It's dreadfully short.'

'And the collar is awful,' said Jessie. 'It looks chewed. Your party one is just as bad though. Whatever happened to the front?'

'Trifle, I think. A long time ago.'

They both sighed, Ermengarde because there was nothing to be done, and Jessica because she was almost sure that her third best Sunday dress which she had never yet worn, and which had been made slightly too large because she didn't really need it, would fit Ermengarde perfectly.

There was nothing little-princess-like about Jessica. She did not enjoy, as Sara had once done, scattering largesse upon the population. She did not even think she should have to, especially when the population was Ermengarde, who chewed things, and the largesse a new dress, dark and light blue silky stripes, with creamy lace at the collar. It took Jessica quite a long time before she could make herself go and collect the blue frock, dump it on Ermengarde's bed, and say, 'There!'

'Oh, Jessie!'

'Don't you dare chew it!'

'I wouldn't! I wouldn't!'

'Take off your school dress, then. Try it on . . . There, I knew it would fit! DON'T DO THAT!'

For Ermengarde, arrayed for the first time in her life in striped blue silk, had burst into tears.

'DON'T, Ermie!' exclaimed Jessica, pushing a pillow into Ermengarde's face in order to blot up the flow. 'Dry up at once, or I'll take it back! Salt water will stain the silk YELLOW!'

Ermengarde, behind her pillow, gave a gasp of horror and dismay and her tears dried up at once.

'I won't borrow it,' she said, speaking (as a precaution against disaster) with the pillow still clamped to her face.

'Of course you will,' said Jessica, irritably, 'but you've *got* to promise that while you're wearing it you won't cry a *single drip*!'

'Are there sad bits in *Peter Pan*?'

'Yes.'

Ermengarde groaned.

'Very sad bits, actually! But you can't cry in them because *if* you do you've got to take off your dress . . . *my* dress, don't forget! Take off my dress . . .'

'*In the middle of the Duke of York's Theatre?*'

'Yes! And watch the rest of the play in your petticoats!'

'Jessie!'

'You just think about that if you feel yourself starting to get tearful!' ordered Jessica. 'That'll stop you!'

'Jessie,' said Ermengarde, barging into her room at bedtime without knocking. 'I just wanted to tell you, if you ever want anything of mine, or want me to help you, or to do anything, *anything*, saving your life or *anything*. I just wanted to say . . . I will.'

But Jessica, who had had enough of heroic behaviour for one day, yawned and continued brushing her hair, and said sleepily, 'Don't be silly, Ermengarde.'

30

From the Outside, Looking In

WHENEVER ERMENGARDE REMEMBERED that Saturday with Aunt Eliza it seemed to her that she had spent the greatest part of it saving herself from crying.

Alice understood why.

'You're all up in the air!' she complained, coming in after breakfast to find Ermengarde with tears in her eyes, fumbling and flustering with her pigtail. 'Whatever has happened to your hair?'

'It's gone all slippery because I washed it.'

'Well, give me the comb and let me sort it! You should be ready! Your aunty's just arrived; she's in the hall waiting. Where's your bag? Are you all packed?'

'Packed?' gasped Ermengarde. She had not thought of packing, nor anything practical.

'Of all the useless misses!' exclaimed Alice impatiently. 'Your hairbrush and your sponge, you want. Your nightdress and a few clean hankies. Your prayerbook for church in the morning and that dress folded up on top so it doesn't crush . . .'

'Oh, I never thought of anything like that!'

'When my little sister,' said Alice, knotting Ermengarde's ribbon into a rock-hard lump, 'was to go and stay with our granny she was packed three weeks before, everything neat as ninepence laid out in that blue and red bag we have, and she wasn't seven years old. Oh, don't start getting weepy! Show me your bag and I'll put your things together while you run down to your aunt. Now what's the matter?'

'Nothing,' said Ermengarde, sniffing and moving as far away as possible from the blue silk dress, just in case any dampness from her should accidentally turn it yellow. 'Will you really pack my things, Alice? You would do it much better than me. Only do you think you could make them into a parcel with some brown paper or something, because I haven't got a bag.'

'Not got a bag! What did you bring your things here in, if you haven't a bag?'

Ermengarde pointed to the huge, brown battered trunk that, being too large to fit under her bed, she used as a window seat.

'Well, you can't take that!' said Alice. 'Your poor aunt would think you were coming to visit for life. Nor are you going off for the weekend with a brown-paper parcel! Never mind! Run down quickly now! I'll find you a bag somewhere.'

Alice was so fast with her packing that she was down in the hall almost before Ermengarde and Aunt Eliza had finished greeting each other. There, she handed to Ermengarde her own beloved red and blue carpetbag, the same one that her little sister had packed so efficiently at the age of not-quite-seven. Ermengarde had seen it often, swinging jauntily from Alice's arm on her days off, or clutched grimly to her chest on the occasions when she took it into her head to frighten the Miss Minchins by handing in her notice. The honour of being allowed to borrow such a treasure brought Ermengarde close to tears again, and she hugged it tightly, and Alice too, saying, 'Oh it's lovely!

Oh, thank you! Oh, you are kind!'

'Very kind,' agreed Aunt Eliza, watching this scene with complete approval. 'Thank you so much! Goodness, how schools have changed since I was a girl! Our mistresses were the most frightening old—'

'Aunt Eliza!' interrupted Ermengarde, hurriedly. 'Alice isn't a teacher or anything! Alice is just Alice! Miss Minchin and Miss Amelia are the teachers here. Miss Amelia isn't what you'd call frightening but Miss Minchin is—'

'Miss Minchin is *here*,' suddenly announced a disapproving voice, and its owner emerged from the shadows of the parlour holding out a large cold hand to Aunt Eliza. 'Alice, return to the kitchen at once and please do not take liberties with the young ladies again! Ermengarde, is something the matter? You look extremely disturbed.'

'No, Miss Minchin,' stammered Ermengarde, realising with a rush of thankfulness that Miss Minchin had only heard the last few words of her speech. 'I am quite well, thank you, Miss Minchin.'

'Then kindly refrain from biting the handles of that bag in such an unladylike manner! I *trust* I can expect you to behave in a fashion befitting a pupil of the Select Seminary while you are with your aunt! In particular, I should like you to remember . . . *Lottie Legh! You naughty child! What do you think you are doing?'*

Ermengarde never found out what it was Miss Minchin particularly wanted her to remember, for at that moment Lottie arrived. Hoping to catch a glimpse of Ermengarde's aunt before they left, she had taken the fastest route to the hall from the second floor, hurtling down the bannisters on her stomach. She hit the newel post at the bottom just as Miss Minchin finished speaking, and tumbled to the floor in a chaos of howls and petticoats. Under cover of the confusion that followed Aunt Eliza and Ermengarde made the sensible but cowardly decision to escape.

'Poor child! We will buy her a present!' said Aunt Eliza, as, pursued by Lottie's shrieks, they fled down the steps to the cab waiting in the square. 'And one for that very nice person who brought your bag, but goodness, your headmistress! Exactly like mine! Oh, Ermengarde, look at the windows!'

'I know!' said Ermengarde, and suddenly tears were pouring down her cheeks again, because the windows of the Select Seminary were full of faces pressed wistfully against the glass, some waving, some still, some pretty, some plain, and none of them smiling.

'We will buy them *all* presents,' promised Aunt Eliza, and Ermengarde mopped her eyes.

And mopped them again when the oculist said, 'Certainly the young lady needs spectacles. I can have some wire frames made up for you for Monday, or tortoiseshells by the end of the week.'

'Not tortoiseshell,' said Ermengarde (miserably mopping), 'because the poor tortoises! How do they . . . no, don't tell me. Are you quite sure I need spectacles, then?'

She was relentlessly informed by the oculist that she certainly did, had probably needed them for years, would almost undoubtedly need them for life, that she should be thankful her problem had been discovered, and that anyway she had two whole days to get used to the idea.

'Sometimes spectacles can look very nice,' Aunt Eliza told her hopefully.

'That's what Jessie said, but all the ones I've ever seen look absolutely dreadful,' said Ermengarde.

Aunt Eliza, the oculist, the oculist's assistant, and the

oculist's secretary, all of them spectacled, kindly pretended not to notice this remark.

Present shopping cheered Ermengarde, as Aunt Eliza had hoped it would. Ermengarde had her pocket money and her birthday sovereign and Aunt Eliza had 'plenty for extras' as she said. They found a little blue cushion with a rabbit on it that was perfect for Lottie, 'Because she came down with such an *awful* bump!' remembered Aunt Eliza, a rainbow of ribbons to brighten the faces at the windows, chocolates for Alice, and an *Elementary Greek Grammar* for Lavinia. ('I am sure Lavinia will be pleased,' remarked Ermengarde, handing over her sovereign. 'She is planning to teach herself Greek as soon as possible.')

There was enough change from the sovereign to buy lovely blue glass beads for Jessica, and some peanuts for Melchisedec, but nothing for Miss Minchin, although Aunt Eliza did suggest it.

'I don't think anyone ever bought a present for Miss Minchin,' said Ermengarde nervously.

After shopping they had lunch, and after lunch they went back to Aunt Eliza's rather gloomy house to change for the theatre.

'This house needs something,' said Aunt Eliza as she took Ermengarde upstairs. 'It is quite a light, bright house, and yet it is dismal. I don't know why.'

'I remember it was much more dismal when Uncle Julius was alive,' said Ermengarde.

'Oh, yes, wasn't it?' agreed Aunt Eliza, and then she and Ermengarde stared at one another, each suddenly quite shocked at the other's truthfulness.

'Ermengarde,' said Aunt Eliza (still in this mood of awful honesty), 'are you happy, dear?'

'Not yet,' said Ermengarde. 'Are you, Aunt Eliza?'

'Not yet,' said Aunt Eliza.

And then they each went to their rooms without saying any more, and when they met again it was as if nothing had happened.

It was Ermengarde's first trip to a theatre. She had watched Punch and Judy shows at children's parties. She had seen a Christmas tableau of angels and shepherds and a stable. Once, during an agonising visit to a friend of her father's, she had been forced to dress herself in bed sheets and play Classical Charades. None of these experiences prepared her in the least for *Peter Pan* at the Duke of

York's Theatre. A wave of magic swept her away. She had come equipped with handkerchiefs, but she lost them during the first interval and did not miss them. At only one moment during the wonderful, mesmerising, astonishing performance was she in any danger of having to take off Jessica's dress and watch the rest of the play in her petticoats.

The moment came right at the end, and surprised her completely. Nana's disgrace, Mrs Darling's tears and even the fading of Tinkerbell had left her sorry but respectably dressed. Captain Hook met his doom. Neverland was left behind and still she was dry-eyed. But when the magic faded, and the heartless Peter Pan flew away, and Wendy was left behind to watch from the window, then Ermengarde suddenly could not bear it.

Too well she understood how Wendy felt. A hotness grew in the back of her eyes, and a terrible fizzing in the top of her nose.

'Oh no!' she moaned in handkerchiefless despair, but she did not forget her promise to Jessie. Tears on the blue silk dress must not happen at any cost. Ermengarde had her sash untied, and several buttons undone before she realised she was recovered again, and understood how right Jessica had been to prescribe undressing in a packed theatre as a cure to excessive sentimentality.

Aunt Eliza (who was wearing her own clothes) wept freely throughout most of the performance, and afterwards asked, 'Wasn't it wonderful?'

'Oh yes! Yes, thank you, Aunt Eliza!'

'But why did you begin to undress at the end?'

'Tears turn blue silk yellow,' Ermengarde explained.

'Ah!' said Aunt Eliza, understandingly.

She and Ermengarde drove away from the threatre in silence, each thinking their own thoughts. Ermengarde kept hers (which were mostly about the heartlessness of Peter) to herself, but Aunt Eliza suddenly said out loud, 'I thought it a great pity that the crocodile escaped!'

And Ermengarde knew that if she was the faithful Wendy, left behind at the window, for Aunt Eliza, Uncle Julius had been the ticking, terrifying crocodile that had pursued her through the years.

Back at Aunt Eliza's, up in her room changing out of Jessica's dress for supper, Ermengarde continued these thoughts.

'Of course, Miss Minchin is a perfect Captain Hook,' she decided. 'And Lavinia and Jessie and the rest are the lost boys. Lottie can be Tinkerbell, and Alice can be Tiger Lily. She would make a very good Indian. Miss Amelia will have to be Nana, I suppose, although she is not really half so sensible. And Sara . . .'

Who was Sara? If she, Ermengarde, was Wendy, forever staring from the window, surely Sara was the heartless person who had left her stranded there?

Alice had packed the red and blue bag very efficiently. Sponge, hairbrush and toothbrush were all together, neatly rolled in a towel. Ermengarde's prayer book and hymn book and clean clothes for morning were underneath. At the bottom was her nightdress case.

There were very few places to put things privately away at the Select Seminary. Drawers and boxes were liable to be pounced on and inspected for tidiness at any time. 'Borrowing' by one's schoolmates was a continual hazard (Gertrude and Lottie in particular were ruthless borrowers). Still, everyone managed to have one small private place for their most secret secrets. At Miss Minchin's the linings of curtains held biscuits, and pillows were stuffed with more than feathers. Soapboxes concealed sweets and pocket money, Jessica's bedsocks held face cream and trinkets and a tiny bottle of perfume, Lavinia's spongebag contained a supply of spare candles for late-night studying, and Ermengarde's nightdress case was stuffed with folded paper.

'Oh!' said Ermengarde, untying the blue ribbons that kept it closed. 'I hope Alice didn't look!'

But of course Alice had not had time to look. 'And anyway, she wouldn't,' said Ermengarde, recovering herself. Alice had simply folded Ermengarde's nightdress and added it on the top. Underneath the contents were quite untouched.

All the letters that Sara had sent to Ermengarde that term.

And, jumbled among them, all the letters that Ermengarde had written, and had not sent, to Sara.

('What?' asked Lottie, when she heard this story. 'All those letters to Sara? You didn't send them?'

'No.'

'Not a single one?'

'No.'

'But you wrote them for her!'

'I wrote them for me.')

Ermengarde, sitting in Aunt Eliza's best spare

bedroom, looking at the collection of unposted letters, told herself rather defensively, 'Well, if I didn't, I didn't.'

But all the same, she turned through the piles of letters from Sara, with the descriptions, the little maps, the shells, and the messages. And all too clearly, she remembered the three unfriendly postcards that had gone back to her friend.

'*Now who's the heartless one?*' asked a little voice in Ermengarde's head.

'Supper in ten minutes,' called Aunt Eliza outside the door.

31

Otherwise Engaged

ERMENGARDE PICKED UP THE LAST LETTER that Sara had written. Between the horror of the prospect of spectacles and the excitement at the thought of the theatre she had forgotten it completely. Now she unfolded the pages again, and looked down at the familiar clear handwriting . . .

We will be coming up to London to get ready . . .

(Becky's wedding, remembered Ermengarde, ashamed. And I was jealous because Sara was making such a fuss of her.)

. . . and as soon as I know the exact day I will write and tell you. But it doesn't matter really because you are always

there, at Miss Minchin's, I mean.

I think it may probably be your last chance to see Becky for quite a while. . .

(I wish I hadn't spent all my money, thought Ermengarde, looking rather regretfully at all the parcels she had bought that morning. I should like to buy Becky a wedding present. Perhaps Aunt Eliza will help me. Where was I?)

. . . last chance to see Becky for quite a while. And me too . . .

Ermengarde read those words again.

And me too

'Sara?' asked Ermengarde, aloud.

And me too, Ermengarde, because you will never guess!

But Ermengarde was beginning to guess.

This is the exciting thing that I mentioned at the beginning of my letter! Uncle Tom and I are going back to India!

Somehow, at the back of Ermengarde's mind, she had

always known that Sara would go back to India one day.

> *As soon as we can get a sailing, Uncle Tom says, because there are businesses to look after there, his own and Papa's, and he has been away too long. Oh, Ermengarde, I have been homesick for India all these years! The sunshine, and the bright flowers and the spicy smell of Indian dust. I shall feel so close to Papa there, too. It makes me feel strange and wonderful inside, just to think of it all. I have been practising my Hindustani with Ram Dass.*
>
> *But I must see you first, Ermie, because it may be a long time before I come back to England again.*
>
> *From Sara, with much love.*

Ermengarde sat in the unfamiliar bedroom of Aunt Eliza's house, staring at Sara's letter, too stunned to think. And then she noticed the letters *PTO* written at the bottom of the page and turned over, and there was a postscript and it was even worse news.

> *Oh, Ermie, I have opened this letter again to tell you more, because we are coming to London on Saturday! This very next Saturday, just for the day! And while Uncle Tom is busy I will be with the Carmichaels, the Large Family, I used to call them, do you remember, on the other side of the square from Miss Minchin's? And then I will see you Ermengarde, because Mrs Carmichael will invite you over to visit and have tea.*

I am sure you will be allowed to come, Ermie, because after all the Carmichaels are neighbours of the Miss Minchins and always see them in church. And the Carmichael girls, Janet and Nora, are just our age and very nice. And so it is quite natural for them to invite you to visit, Ermengarde, but Uncle Tom says that perhaps it would be easier for everyone if Miss Minchin did not know that I would be there too.

And that will make it completely reasonable for her to say 'Yes'.

And I am sure she will.

She must.

It is wonderful to think I will see you again so soon.

Sara.

'Aunt Eliza,' cried Ermengarde, flying down the stairs. 'I must go back! I must go back to Miss Minchin's now, at once, very quickly!'

'Ermengarde!'

'I found a letter from someone,' said Ermengarde distractedly, 'a letter I hadn't read. And it was from Sara, my best friend Sara! And she wants to see me now, today, because after today she is sailing to India. I'm sorry, Aunt Eliza, and there are lots of things I wish I could talk to you about but I can't just now, you see, because I haven't time, Oh, please would you let me go back to school? And would you not tell Miss Minchin and Miss Amelia why you have brought me?'

'But . . .'

'*Please*, Aunt Eliza?' begged Ermengarde, and started crying again.

Perhaps Aunt Eliza recognised desperation when she saw it, because she abandoned the roast chicken ordered especially for Ermengarde's supper and did exactly as she asked. Half an hour later they were back outside the Select Seminary, gazing from the window of their cab at its large, unwelcoming black door.

'Perhaps I can sneak in without anyone noticing,' said Ermengarde hopefully. 'Then I won't have to answer lots of questions about why I came back so early. And if anyone does ask I shall say . . . I shall say . . . What *shall* I say, Aunt Eliza?'

'Say,' said Aunt Eliza, after a long moment of thought, 'Aunt Eliza thought it best.'

And as she watched Ermengarde climb the steps to the Select Seminary's door she hoped that this was true. It was such a big door, and Ermengarde looked so alone.

And then Aunt Eliza relaxed a little, because after all Ermengarde was not alone. She had been joined by a large black cat. Aunt Eliza watched as her niece bent to stroke it, and then smiled as the cat slid in after her through the closing Seminary door.

After that Aunt Eliza waited for quite a long time, 'In case they come out again,' as she told the cab driver, but neither Ermengarde nor the cat reappeared.

Ermengarde was lucky. Neither of the Miss Minchins noticed her return. Alice did, and she received the explanation, 'Aunt Eliza thought it best,' with raised eyebrows and reproachful shakings of her head, assuming that Ermengarde had behaved so badly that this was the natural result.

The schoolroom (who had enjoyed a very exciting afternoon) guessed otherwise.

'You are back because of Sara, aren't you?' asked Gertrude eagerly. 'Oh, Ermengarde, it has been so exciting! First, Mrs Carmichael, you know the fat lady with the hundreds of children, came with a note to invite you over for the afternoon. Alice took it in to Miss Minchin, and we got out of her afterwards that the note had said that she would like you to meet her girls and stay to tea. And Miss Minchin told Alice to say that the reply was thank you but certainly not! And that anyway, the young lady in question was otherwise engaged.'

'You were otherwise engaged watching *Peter Pan*, you see,' put in Lottie, enviously. 'So then, after Mrs Carmichael had been sent away, guess what . . .'

'The Indian gentleman!' burst in Jessica. 'You know, Ermie, the one that Sara calls Uncle Tom! He came! But he had no luck either! We heard Miss Amelia telling Alice that Miss Minchin was lying down with one of her dreadful heads, and that any callers should be told that the Miss Minchins were not at home to visitors . . .'

'So he slunk away too . . .'

'Slunk?'

'Well, walked rather quickly. And then . . .'

'And then . . . and then . . .' shouted Lottie, jumping up and down, 'SARA came!'

'Oh!'

'Yes, all by herself!' said Jessica, taking up the story. 'We all saw her! We were watching out of the window. And Miss Amelia must have been watching too, because before Sara even got to the front doorstep Miss Amelia rushed into the square and stopped her coming any closer. So then Lottie . . .'

'I'm telling it now!' interrupted Lottie. '*I* sneaked

down to Alice's room and Alice's window was wide open like I knew it would be because she likes plenty of fresh air like everyone has in Epping, and I could hear Miss Amelia, *plain as plain*, Ermengarde, telling Sara that you were away for the whole weekend! And Sara stood very still and straight, like a soldier, looking at Miss Amelia, while Miss Amelia fussed and flapped all over the pavement and said over and over again how you were not here, until at last Sara said, "I see. Thank you, Miss Amelia," and turned away.

'And she looked dreadfully sad, Ermie.'

32

Being a Beast

THAT EVENING ERMENGARDE WAS TOO
miserable to sleep, or even rest. Instead she wrapped the
blue cloak around her, picked up Melchisedec's peanuts
and crept up to the attic to confess her sins. The brown-
paper peanut bag was not very strong, and because of
this Ermengarde did not arrive as quietly as usual.
Melchisedec was scurrying back towards his hole in
alarm as she came through the door.

'Don't run away, Melchisedec,' she begged. 'I didn't
mean to startle you. You only heard some peanuts I
dropped. I have been awful, Melchisedec! I have been
a beast!'

If Melchisedec was shocked he managed not to show

it. Instead he came bravely forward and picked up one of the fallen nuts.

'I sulked,' continued Ermengarde miserably, huddling on to the bed with her hands clasped round her knees. 'I sulked because of the magic. You know, the magic that changed this attic into that little fairy-tale room. I saw it. Lavinia saw it. You must have seen it, too.'

Melchisedec, who was good at keeping secrets, gave her an inscrutable glance, neither admitting nor denying it.

'We weren't meant to, though. It was private magic, for Sara. For Sara and Becky,' admitted Ermengarde, acknowledging at last this most uncomfortable truth of all. 'They were the ones that needed it. I understand that now.'

Ermengarde sighed, and Melchisedec (who had begun to gobble nuts at a tremendous rate) glanced up and looked encouragingly sympathetic.

'But I didn't see that before,' Ermengarde went on. 'I sulked because Sara didn't share, and I have sulked ever since. I wrote answers to her letters, but only to make myself feel better. I never posted a single one. And I have been terribly jealous of Becky. (I always was a little bit jealous of poor Becky, you know.) I have thought horrible things, and not been nice about the presents Sara sent (Lottie wrote those thank-you cards, really, not me). Do you know, I didn't even bother to finish reading the last letter Sara wrote? And she came here, Melchisedec, 'specially to see me, and I didn't know until it was too late!'

Ermengarde sniffed dismally.

'And now she is going to India, and when will I see her again? Lottie said . . .' (Ermengarde gulped, and Melchisedec did too, perhaps in sympathy) '. . . Lottie said she looked dreadfully sad.'

Then Ermengarde put her head in her hands and had a long, damp, sniffly, remorseful weep. Melchisedec was dreadfully bored, but it did Ermengarde good. When she finally stopped she was cold and exhausted but strangely calm. She was also so tired that if she had been a little more comfortable she would have been fast asleep.

'I must go to bed,' she said blurrily to Melchisedec.

She left the attic in a dozy, dreamlike state. At the foot of the stairs she stumbled and almost fell. It took her a minute or two to gather herself up, and then, quite suddenly she was at her bedroom door, and then she was in bed, and the day with all its tears and troubles was over, and the darkness was like water soaking into her bones, and she was tumbling and floating and drowning in sleep. She had lost the blue cloak, but she did not know.

Miss Minchin knew. She found it.

'I knew,' she whispered. 'I knew, I knew, I knew . . .'

'Very likely you did,' agreed Alice, who was already in her nightgown, having developed the cosy but outrageously unmaidlike habit of undressing for bed in front of the last of the schoolroom fire. 'You need to drink a pint of cold water, ma'am, and take yourself off for a good night's sleep. That cloak wants airing, if you don't mind me saying. It smells fusty. Were you thinking of wearing it?'

'You must not touch it,' said Miss Minchin.

'Suit yourself,' replied Alice cheerfully.

'It belongs to that girl.'

'Which one would that be, then?' enquired Alice, yawning hugely without covering her mouth.

'That mischief-making, deceitful, secretive, mocking . . .'

'Goodness!' said Alice. 'If you think our young ladies are trouble you should see some of the madams we have to concern ourselves about in Epping! I will go to my bed now, miss, if there's nothing you need. Sunday boots to sort out in the morning, and by the way, I've told the young ladies they are as capable of boot cleaning as I am. I've arranged for them to come down to the scullery in twos . . .'

'. . . Sara Crewe!' said Miss Minchin, but Alice, the only person at the Select Seminary who had absolutely no interest in Sara Crewe, was already out of the door.

Bosco was put out.

'Out!' they had commanded, and pushed him on to the doorstep, not kicked exactly, but definitely nudged with their feet. It was not his fault; he had been ill. Sick, in fact, on the front doormat. Careless people had trodden it all over the house.

Now there was a very strong smell. That cod's head he'd had for his supper must have been off, they said. Out you go, Bosco! Hurry! Don't let him slide past you up the stairs! Grab him by the scruff! Quick, he's coughing again! Out! Get some fresh air!

Bosco did not like fresh air. He liked warm, fuggy air, especially the air of the Select Seminary, with its lingering fragrances of wonderful food. However, unluckily for him, it was an extremely cold evening; so cold that Alice had closed her bedroom window. Bosco was terribly shocked when he discovered that. Windows were the best ways he knew of getting in and out of houses. Doors were much more chancey things. Doors were like birds, unpredictable and flapping. They required patience and pouncing skills and alertness and concentration. Bosco was a lazy cat. He had quickly given up wasting such vast amounts of efforts on the sparrows of the squares: such feathery, tickling mouthfuls weren't worth the trouble. But the door of the Seminary was a different matter. Bosco positioned himself at the foot of the steps and prepared to wait.

How fortunate it was for Bosco that Ermengarde had embroidered that hideous tablecloth! If she had not, Aunt Eliza would never have sent the message concerning the oculist which alarmed Ermengarde so much that Sara's letter was entirely disregarded, stuffed into a nightdress case, and forgotten. Forgotten, that was, until Alice efficiently packed the case into the red and blue bag, where it was discovered by Ermengarde.

She and Bosco had been overcome at almost exactly the same moment, Bosco by the fish head, Ermengarde by remorse.

How could I have been so deceived? thought Bosco

How could I have been so unkind? wailed Ermengarde, remembering her heartless treatment of Sara ever since her inadvertent discovery of the transformation of the attic long ago, in the days before Christmas when the brass plate had shone so brightly and the Select Seminary front steps were the cleanest in the square, and Alice was still in Epping, and Oxford, as far as anyone at Miss Minchin's knew or cared, was no more than a ridiculous place to think of buying a hat.

Bosco had undone his deception on the doormat with all possible speed. Ermengarde, with equal urgency, had begged to be taken back to the Select Seminary in the hope of seeing her friend one last time. They had met on the doorstep and entered together. Ermengarde had disappeared into the schoolroom, Bosco had fled down the kitchen stairs.

He had taken refuge in Alice's room. His plan was to stay concealed until the inhabitants of the house went to bed, and then, by stealthy, catlike ways, to find a warm place and go to sleep in it. He hoped to avoid the Young Ladies if he could; he did not wish to be hugged and stroked. He was far from fully recovered from his encounter with the cod.

That was Bosco's plan, he fell asleep thinking of it, and when he awoke the house was quiet and dark, and the bed above him was sagging almost to the floor and making rhythmic snorting sounds, which meant that Alice was in it and asleep.

Time to explore, thought Bosco.

The way from the basement to the rest of the house was up the kitchen stairs and through a door at the back of the hall, which the Miss Minchins were always closing and Alice was always leaving open. It was open now, so Bosco wandered through, inspected the dining room (cold and empty) and the parlour (cold and stuffy), avoided the stairs that led to the bedrooms (he was still feeling antisocial) and finally settled on the schoolroom as the place to spend the night.

The schoolroom fire had dwindled to grey embers, but that did not worry Bosco, because he had developed a method for dealing with such problems.

Bosco could light fires by willpower. He could also fill food dishes and empty his favourite chair by the same useful force. His method was simple: he sat and gazed at the object to be controlled. It always worked; sooner or later, some human slave would come along and notice his implacable, golden stare.

At this point Bosco would speak his only word.

'Woe!' he would say (mournfully), and the human slave would immediately and apologetically cry: 'Oh, Bosco! Poor old Bosco! Have you been waiting long?'

And they would rush to obey his command.

Bosco sat on the schoolroom hearthrug, as close as he could get to the fender, and gazed at the cold cinders in the grate and willed them to burst into warmth and comfort. He was not unhappy. Sooner or later, he was perfectly certain, an obedient human would appear.

Late as it was, the house was still not quite asleep. Lavinia was awake, poring over the prospectus of a North London school. It seemed to be an institution as unlike the Select Seminary as it was possible to imagine. The back pages gave a list of recent achievements of Old Girls. There were not only university students, teachers and nurses, but also translators, and scientists, doctors and writers. Someone was excavating the ruins of Herculaneum, another was a journalist.

'Expert in the design of stained-glass windows . . .' read Lavinia, amazed. 'Horticulture . . . Dentist . . . Rabbit farmer . . . Association of Women Pharmacists'

No faces at the Select Seminary windows were ever as wistful as Lavinia's as she looked out into that new world.

Melchisedec was also awake, surveying with indignation his second visitor of the night. Who was this large, bony, odd-smelling person? he silently demanded. What whispers of maids, and chatters of schoolgirls, and memories of uncovered secrets had led her to his attic? Why did she clutch that cloak? Did she imagine it would lure him into believing that she was the gentle Ermengarde who brought him such quantities of wonderful food? For what reason had she pounced so eagerly on his last and largest peanut, with the triumphant cry of, 'Here's another!' And if she was as hungry as she appeared, why had she not immediately eaten it? And who was she waiting for, in that chair pushed back in the shadows?

'I'll wait,' she had said, and blown out the candle. A little later her voice had come out of the darkness to add, 'It was here that I caught them before.'

'Go away!' Melchisedec silently commanded, but she leaned her head against the wall and fell asleep.

If she stays forever, thought Melchisedec, I shall move. Live elsewhere. Leave, as did my wife and children. Next door perhaps. The attic there is no longer deserted, I know. A person visits it from time to time. Where there are people there will always be food. The person is a boy with hair like flames. His hearing is acute, but he is not listening for rats . . .

('Ghosts,' the hopeful red-headed boy Tristram had explained to Bosco. 'They have them next door, so why not here? What could be more educational than a spot of ghost-watching?')

However, continued the musing Melchisedec, before I move next door I must consider That Cat . . .

Miss Minchin gave a sudden snore and dropped the peanut; the last of the trail of peanuts that had led her to that place.

Mine! thought Melchisedec, and grabbed it.

33

Never You Do That

BOSCO'S LONG WAIT WAS NEARLY OVER.
Lottie's eiderdown tumbled on to the floor, kicked off in
a dream of bannister sliding, and she found herself
suddenly awake. All around her were shadowy humps
that were her room-mates, buried so deeply under the
covers that even their heads did not stick out.
Hibernating, thought Lottie, like animals in caves.

She did not feel a bit like hibernating herself; she felt
wide awake and bright with mischief. For a little while,
she had the world to herself.

The night before, under Miss Amelia's supervision,
Sunday clothes had been laid out on bedside chairs,
ready for morning. Silently Lottie set about livening up

that dull day, creeping from chair to chair to turn dresses inside out, redistribute petticoats and underwear to new, different-sized owners, and knot everyone's Sunday stockings into a long, thick black rope. After which she refreshed herself with a biscuit from her curtain-hem-biscuit-supply, noticed with pleasure that it was snowing, and tiptoed out of the door.

Dare I slide down the bannisters in the dark? she wondered, decided she dared, and did it.

The hall was not quite as dark as the rest of the house; there was a street lamp outside, and it shone through the fanlight above the Select Seminary's front door. It lit the hands of the grandfather clock.

'Half past two,' read Lottie, and was so surprised to discover that it was not, as she had supposed, early morning, that she tiptoed across the hall to check the time on the schoolroom clock.

And there, on the hearthrug, sat Bosco.

When Bosco knew that he had a human audience at last he willed the fire alight more strongly than ever, staring with unwavering eyes at the spot from which the flames should spring, and he spoke his word of command.

'Woe!' said Bosco.

'Oh, Bosco! Poor old Bosco!' cried Lottie (as they always did). 'Have you been waiting long?'

Thanks to her early-morning lessons with Alice, Lottie knew all about lighting fires. From the sifting of the ashes to the striking of the match, she knew exactly how it should be done. Also she knew about the small, damp-smelling cupboard beside the hearth where the newspapers and kindling and matches were kept. Nor did she forget the magic ingredient of a splash of lamp oil from the lamp in the hall. That lamp was a treasure, an heirloom of the house of Minchin, fluted glass and heavy brass.

'I'd better be careful,' said Lottie.

Carefully she removed the pearly shade and the glass chimney. Carefully she carried the heavy base with its reservoir of paraffin into the schoolroom. Carefully she added the splash of oil to her beautifully laid grate, several splashes actually, an accidental puddle in the hearth, and a trail of drips leading back through the schoolroom to the hall again. Carefully she replaced the chimney and the fluted shade.

And then the lamp was safely back on its table, looking

like it had never been touched, and Lottie found she had been holding her breath all the while.

'Never you do that!' she said feelingly to Bosco.

Lottie's fire was the best fire that ever warmed the perpetually chilly Select Seminary. One match was all it took, jabbed into the centre of the rolled paper and kindling. If Lottie had jabbed a sleeping dragon it could not have been more successful. It exploded into life with a dragon-sized roar, leaped from the hearth and began its raging journey.

Lottie and Bosco fled shrieking before it.

The stairs became impossible in less than two minutes.

Dramas erupted all over the house.

'It wasn't my fault!' wailed Lottie, shaking in Lavinia's furious grip. 'I only did what Alice did! Don't tell Miss Minchin!'

The grandfather clock in the hall, dry, seasoned oak and walnut, well coated with a hundred years' worth of inflammable wood polish (although very little had been added since Alice's arrival), rushed into flame without a moment's hesitation, struck one last time, burst open and crashed to the ground, right above Cook and Alice's heads.

'Something went bump,' murmured Cook, and turned over in her sleep.

Alice woke more thoroughly. She sat up, sniffed, jumped out of bed and ran up the kitchen stairs. For a fraction of time she stared through the door that led into the hall. She saw nothing but fire. She turned, slammed the door and flew back down the stairs and dragged Cook out of bed.

Cook, once she understood that the house was on fire, was utterly useless.

'I allus knew that range would do for me!' she moaned.

'It's not the range!' shouted Alice. 'It's upstairs, in the hall, and all those girls asleep above! I'm going to try and get up to them again. You go out through the kitchen and wake the square!'

But Cook could not seem to understand this simple instruction. She refused to go out by the kitchen and insisted on climbing through her bedroom window instead, and once she was safely out she did not wake anyone. Instead she sat on the front doorstep, rocking to and fro and whimpering. It was Alice, who after a second brave attempt to get up the stairs to the hall, began to wake the square.

'Fire!' she cried, hammering on doors and shrieking at windows, and at last people began to emerge.

34

The Only Way Out

EVERYONE SAID AFTERWARDS THAT Lavinia was marvellous. Once she understood what was happening she rushed among the older girls, quelling panic and issuing orders.

'Wet towels over faces!' she commanded. 'They will filter the smoke. Soak them in your water jugs and tie them on tight. Oh, for goodness sake, Gertrude! Drips don't matter! Don't try and rescue things! Leave everything behind! Close the doors; it slows fire down! Upstairs! Get the little ones out of bed and count them! Ermengarde, *wake up*!'

Miss Amelia's bedroom was at the back of the house. It

had a door opening into her sister's, an unprivate arrangement that she had always resented. Unprivate or not, it saved her life, because Miss Minchin's room opened in turn to the parlour, and that meant that Miss Amelia could reach the parlour window without entering the blazing hall. And then, theoretically, she was safe because below the parlour window stood a circle of seven valiant neighbours holding a blanket, all ready to catch her. Nor was it a very big jump.

But Miss Amelia wouldn't.

'Leave everything behind!' Lavinia had ordered. It was easier said than done. Gertrude's money box contained two years' worth of hoarded shillings and sixpences; one day, she believed, they would become a bicycle. That was why, despite the smoke billowing through the house, and the terrifying sounds from downstairs, she wasted thirty seconds dragging aside her bed and prising up her secret floorboard. She was not the only one. Lavinia herself had her new Greek Grammar. Others clutched their Christmas lockets, battered dolls, photographs in silver frames. One girl carried a stained and heavy writing case, like a little desk without legs.

'You can't!' snapped Lavinia.

'I must, it was my brother's.'

'He'll understand.'

'He's dead.'

They took an end each and raced up the stairs, choking despite the wet towels, eyes smarting and streaming tears. In the little ones' dormitory the air was clearer, however. Lavinia ordered more wet towel tying and counted heads. Twelve, and Bosco.

'Jessie and Ermengarde?' she demanded. 'Where are they? I saw them a minute ago! Have they gone back?'

'We're here,' panted Jessica, and she and Ermengarde came gasping through the door in a cloud of smoke. Each carried an armload of dresses. Ermengarde had not forgotten her offer to repay Jessica for the loan of the blue silk dress. As soon as Lavinia had shaken her awake she had dashed off to Jessica's room, fully prepared to save her life. She had found herself saving her wardrobe instead.

'Now I don't have to choose!' said Jessica thankfully, and bundled her arms full of frocks.

Without Lavinia, everyone would have been too panic-stricken to think ahead at all. Even as it was, some of the little ones were frantic.

'What are we going to do?' they begged. 'We can't stay here! There are bars on the windows! Why doesn't anyone come? Where's Alice? Won't there be a fire engine? Oh, Lavvie, *do something*!'

'Up to the attics,' ordered Lavinia. 'Fast but no pushing! Ermengarde, show them the way! The only way out is up.'

Miss Amelia was still dithering.

'Jump!' called her rescuers, eight of them now because they had been joined by the vicar.

'I can't find my sister!'

'The fire brigade will take care of her,' they cried back (although there was no sign of the fire brigade at all at that moment). 'Jump, Miss Amelia, while there is still time!'

'Take courage, dear lady,' added the vicar. 'Climb on to the windowsill and propel yourself outwards as far as you are able.'

This was a dreadfully hard order for poor Miss Amelia to follow. The encouraging words 'dear lady' got her as far as the windowsill, but propelling herself outwards as far as she was able was quite another matter, not least because she was, as she wailed to the circle around the blanket, far from suitably dressed.

('And what,' enquired Miss Minchin, some years later, 'would you consider suitable dress for jumping from a parlour window in the middle of the night? I cannot think of anything in your wardrobe at that time which would have improved your situation!'

'There is now,' said Miss Amelia, who had come on immensely.)

All the time Miss Amelia dithered, the fire grew stronger. The schoolroom windows shattered and poured out orange flames and then reeking black smoke as the ceiling collapsed. The staircase became a blazing scaffold, leaning drunkenly over the dining room door. Outside, the heat and smoke were making it harder and harder for the blanket holders to stay close to the house. The vicar begged despairingly, 'Jump, dearest Amelia, for my sake!' and at the same moment the parlour door split from top to bottom.

'Close your eyes!' cried Miss Amelia, and jumped at last.

* * *

The attic rooms were eerily quiet. The two closed doors
at the head and foot of the attic stairs muffled the sounds
from beneath. The girls themselves were silent from the
shock of finding Miss Minchin fast asleep and snoring,
her head still propped against the wall of Sara's room,
her hands still gripping the old blue cloak. One by
one they had reached the top of the stairs and stopped
dead with surprise as they took in the sight through
the open door.

'Don't wake her!' Lavinia had ordered, and beckoned
them away to gather in Becky's old room.

'But we can't leave her to die!' protested Lottie, still
clutching Bosco.

'No one is going to die!' snapped Lavinia. 'There's a
way out of the house from up here! Ermengarde knows
it . . . Yes, you do, Ermengarde! Why are you staring
like that?'

Ermengarde was staring because she was utterly
bewildered.

'There's no way out,' she faltered. 'Why do you think
I know a way out? How could there be, from right
up here?'

'Of course there's a way out!' said Lavinia. 'There's some way of getting through to next door. There must be! How did all those things get here otherwise?'

'Lavinia! What things?'

'Sara's things of course! All that stuff we saw that night last term! Tables and rugs and books and dishes! Lamps and quilts and flowers! Cushions! They didn't come through *this* house; Miss Minchin would have seen.'

'I thought . . .' began the astounded Ermengarde, 'I thought it was . . . magic . . .'

Even as she spoke she was ashamed. Thirteen years old, and believing in magic! 'I don't know . . . I didn't think. How else . . .'

'Ermengarde, how can you be so silly! They were Indian things! They came from the Indian gentleman next door! There must be a way between the houses . . . some little hidden connecting passage? *Think!*'

'I *can't*,' wailed Ermengarde desperately, but of course she could. The answer was easy, once you stopped believing in magic.

'The monkey came over the roof,' she said, at last. 'There's a skylight in Sara's room. Sara used to climb up on the table and push it open to feed the sparrows.

So did I sometimes. There's a skylight next door too, quite close. But even if we could get to it, how could we open it?'

'Smash it,' said Lavinia, briskly. 'And then use Jessie's dresses to cover over the sharp bits. Just the thing! Shut up, Jess!'

'The roof slopes . . .'

'Come on!'

'We haven't even a rope . . .'

The quietest of the little ones produced the chain of knotted stockings.

'Miss Minchin is in there! She will never let us!'

'We'll go very quietly and wake her up last.'

'But it's *dangerous*!' wailed Ermengarde.

'Ermengarde,' said Lavinia. 'The house is on fire! I'll go first.'

At half past two that morning Lottie had slid down the bannisters. At a quarter to three she set the house on fire. By three o'clock Alice and Cook were in the square. At a quarter past three Miss Amelia jumped, for the vicar's sake, into a blanket held by the neighbours. Two fire engines arrived at this time also, and began pouring water through the blazing parlour window. Five minutes after that, Miss Amelia was being comforted by Alice and Cook. She would have preferred being comforted by the vicar, but he had hurried around to the back of the house where several neighbours, including Mr Carmichael and the Indian gentleman, the red-headed boy and his uncle, were attempting to reach the first-floor windows.

Miss Amelia's room was alight now, and the smoke was hot and blinding. Nobody had a high enough ladder. The red-headed boy's uncle was savage with helplessness. The red-headed boy was red-headed no longer. All his hair was singed off, and his eyebrows as well. He had tried to get in by the kitchen and been dragged out seconds before the ceiling collapsed. He had been pulled away from the drainpipe too, which perhaps was lucky because a moment later it had fallen as well.

'You are nothing but an infernal young nuisance!' roared his uncle at this point. 'Take yourself off!'

Tristram took himself back to the square, which was now in complete confusion, made worse by the presence of children everywhere. The Carmichael offspring, escaped from their bedrooms and nurseries. The little ragged girls who sold flowers outside the church. The grey, cold scullery maids who scrubbed steps in the mornings. They milled around, shrieking and pointing, racing for a better view. They were under everyone's feet until a huge policeman suddenly bellowed, 'SOMEONE GET THESE YOUNG ONES INSIDE!' and in order to demonstrate exactly what he meant, grabbed Tristram by the shoulders and marched him to the Carmichaels' front door.

'I'm not a child!' protested Tristram, twisting in the policeman's grip. 'I'm a *student*! Let me go! I don't even live here! I live in the house next door to the fire!'

'CHILDREN INSIDE!' bellowed the policeman, completely ignoring him. 'Now! All of you!'

And to Mrs Carmichael and other distracted females clustering helplessly around, 'Can't you women do something? Good Lord, and you want to be given the vote!'

He gave Tristram a final shove and hurried back to the fire, but his words worked wonders. In no time his outraged listeners got to work. Only by ducking into the shadow of a wall did Tristram escape the indignant shepherding towards open doors. Even so, he was not completely unobserved. As he slid out of sight he felt a clutch on his arm and heard a voice, very clear, very desperate, saying, 'The attic! The attic! You said you lived in the house next door. Tell them there's a way out through the attic! Tell someone!'

The clutching hand was pulled away then as the last of the children were herded inside.

'Tell someone!' repeated the voice, high and frightened. 'Run!'

Tristram ran, not to tell someone; having been sent away twice, bellowed at, shoved and marched away with the children, he had no hope of being listened to by anyone any more. Instead he ran towards his own front door, and by great good luck he arrived at the moment when one of the fire engine horses began to struggle and panic. Nobody noticed as he slipped inside.

At half past three in the morning Lavinia stood on the table in the little attic bedroom that had once belonged to Sara, and pushed open the skylight. A gale of smoke-filled, snow-flecked, ice-cold air poured into the attic.

Miss Minchin stirred and lifted her head.

Lavinia clambered on to the roof.

'Pass me one of your dresses, Jessie,' she hissed.

'Which one?'

'The thickest.'

'But that's my pink velvet!'

'Perfect. And one end of the stocking rope. You hold the other, very tight.'

'Are you all right?'

'Of course,' said Lavinia, and with the stocking rope tied round her waist and the pink velvet dress wrapped round her neck, she crawled on hands and knees, across the slippery, sloping tiles under an orange, smoke-filled sky.

It was snowing black snow.

Tristram opened his skylight window just as Lavinia (with her hand prudently wrapped in Jessica's pink velvet frock) raised her *Elementary Greek Grammar* to smash it.

'Getting a bit hot at the Pudding Shop?' said Tristram.

35

No More Miss Minchin's

THEY FLED THE BURNING HOUSE LIKE sparrows caught before a storm; anxious, wind-buffeted, exclaiming and cheeping in voices that blew away in the night.

'Tie that to something!' Lavinia ordered Tristram, handing him the end of the stocking rope. 'It's not very strong, but it will be better than nothing. I'm sending the little ones first. Help them over and count them! There should be eight.'

'Eight. All right.'

'And take care of this dress! Don't dump it where it will be trodden on. It's pink velvet.'

'Pink velvet. Absolutely.'

'Here's Lottie coming now. If I stay halfway to steady her, can you lift her down?'

'Of course! Hullo, Lottie! Whoa, Bosco!'

Bosco was the first to escape, shooting recklessly across the tiles past Lottie and swerving round Tristram as if he were afraid he might send him back. Lottie followed after him only slightly less slowly, and after that a pattern began. Jessica and Ermengarde stood on the table and boosted people on to the roof. Lavinia met them halfway. Tristram, sprawled precariously on his front, stretched across the slippery tiles as far as he could reach, hauled people in and lowered them through his open window.

Miss Minchin, although she did not intend it, was the greatest help of all. Her appalling presence quelled any thought of disorder or hysterics.

'Scream, and she will notice you!' hissed Gertrude terrifyingly to the little ones, and that threat was enough to make the rescue possible.

'Think if they had started panicking or crying!' said Jessica, afterwards. 'We could never have managed! Think if it had been Cook in the attic with us . . .'

'She'd have stuck in the skylight.'

'Or Alice!'

'Alice would have made us all jump off the roof,' said Gertrude. 'I can just imagine it! "No time for fussing around crawling over tiles. Off the roof, double quick, we do it all the time in Epping!"'

'Think if it had been *Miss Amelia*!'

'I know. It would have been exactly like being trapped in a burning attic with a gigantic, alive, lunatic roasting chicken!'

'Thank goodness it was Miss Minchin!'

'Thank goodness.'

And yet Miss Minchin did nothing. Her house burned beneath her, her pupils took flight from above her head, and she sat silent in her chair in the shadows. Only her eyes showed that she was aware of her surroundings. Her dark hooded gaze was alarmed and disbelieving, like a person watching a nightmare unfold from their dreams. . Once she half stood, as if suddenly startled, but Ermengarde said nervously, 'It's all right, Miss Minchin,' and she resumed her seat again.

('She was in shock,' Alice diagnosed afterwards. 'It happened just the same to my grandad once, back home in Epping.'

'Did his house burn down?'

'No, but a pig ate his wallet. It was much the same.')

The eight little ones were rescued in less than eight minutes, and because Lottie and Bosco had crossed so easily, and Lavinia was so bossy, and Tristram so cheerful, they were safe before they had a chance to become any more frightened. Once they were across the elder girls followed, and when finally the attic was almost empty, even the desk and the dresses rescued, Lavinia crawled back across the tiles to see how Ermengarde and Jessica were managing.

'She hasn't said a word,' whispered Jessica, glancing over her shoulder at the silent presence in the corner.

'Never mind. You climb out now, Jess. Tristram is waiting for you. I will manage Miss Minchin. Ermengarde will help.'

Jessica scrambled out very thankfully, and a moment later Lavinia dropped down beside Ermengarde on the table. As she landed, something in the house below them fell. There was rumbling, rushing sound, the walls trembled and the floor was suddenly not level but slanting.

'*Lavinia!*' squeaked Ermengarde.

Lavinia was already beside Miss Minchin, had taken her hands and was urging her to her feet.

'There's no time left,' Ermengarde heard her say, but talking quite calmly, leading her towards the skylight as she spoke. 'Come on, Miss Minchin. We have to go!'

Then they heard Miss Minchin's voice at last, a croaking single word, 'Amelia?'

'She's quite safe,' said Lavinia. 'The boy next door saw her in the square. Cook and Alice too. And all the girls are out now. We are the only ones left. Take her other arm, Ermie, and we'll get her up to the window.'

For Ermengarde, that moment of touching Miss Minchin's arm was the most frightening part of the whole dreadful night. It was like laying her hand on something dangerous and forbidden; a blade or a wound or a caged, unknown creature. She had to tell herself, "It's just a sleeve. It's just a sleeve", before she could make herself obey. And yet Lavinia, on Miss Minchin's other side, had her arm right around her, and was helping her climb, steadying her, saying, 'I'm right beside you . . . I won't let go . . . Here's Tristram to help you too,' calling back over her shoulder, 'Ermie, follow straight away! Hurry!'

'I'm coming now!' replied Ermengarde, and from the sounds all around her, she knew she must. All the same, for one minute more she stood alone in the little attic room. Her eyes stung with fire and tears. Every breath of the dreadful, dark air was sore in her lungs. Her throat hurt so much she could hardly whisper.

'Melchisedec.'

He came straight away, recognising her as the only familiar object left in his whole calamitous world. She scooped him up and wrapped him tightly in her old red woolly shawl. The floor shifted again, with a dreadful sawing, grinding sound. Tiles began to clatter on the roof outside. She heard a scream, and Tristram's voice, very close, asking, 'Where's the goldy one?'

Then his and Lavinia's outstretched hands were reaching down to help her, and she climbed out of the window and into the night, and very soon after that there was no more Miss Minchin's.

36

Five O'clock in the Morning

THE ARRIVAL INTO THE SQUARE OF THE girls from Miss Minchin's caused pandemonium. They tumbled gasping from Tristram's front door and seemed to fall straight into a hundred clutching arms. They were wept over, blessed, counted, scolded, questioned and hugged, not once or twice, but over and over, by firemen, neighbours, most of the congregation of St Stephen's, Sara (who had watched in agony from the Carmichaels' drawing room window after she had been pulled away), and all the little grey shapeless girls who scrubbed steps without coats on freezing mornings.

Tristram's uncle said, 'Perhaps after all there is a God.' The vicar, who had never doubted it, knelt in the mud and ashes, and gave thanks. Cook remarked that it was the kitchen range that had done it, and she had always known it would. Bosco discovered an open door, wandered inside, and began to concentrate his powers on another empty grate.

Ermengarde and Sara fell into one another's arms and the first thing Ermengarde said was, 'I've got Melchisedec!'

'Oh, Ermengarde!' sobbed Sara, and then for a long time they hugged each other and wept and hugged each other and laughed and hugged each and exclaimed, 'Oh, Sara! Oh, Ermie!' until Melchisedec began to think he could endure it no longer.

Something must be done, he thought. I shall act! And he bit a hole in Ermengarde's shawl.

The view he gained of the seething gas-lit square changed his mind very quickly.

Surrounded by enemies, he diagnosed, after one bulging-eyed, horrified glance, and curled up very small and round, like a homeless little animal with nowhere left to run.

At five o'clock in the morning, kind Mrs Carmichael, by

putting her boys to sleep on the floor, packing the little ones in head to toe, and turning her own bedroom over to the Miss Minchins, managed to send the entire Select Seminary to bed.

Although not immediately to sleep.

In every room, it seemed, there was something that must be said. Lottie, for example, tucked up on the sofa in the study with Mrs Carmichael for company, had something on her mind.

'Nobody should blame Bosco,' she said.

'Nobody does,' replied Mrs Carmichael soothingly.

'Or Alice.'

'No. Nor Alice.'

'Though she did show me how to light a fire!'

'Don't worry, Lottie. Nobody is blaming Alice,' murmured Mrs Carmichael.

Lottie seemed less comforted than ever.

'Who are you blaming then? Who are you blaming then?' she wailed unhappily.

'Nobody is blaming anyone,' said Mrs Carmichael (for perhaps the twentieth time).

Gertrude also had worries.

'Where,' she asked, of the three nearly-fast-asleep

people in her room, 'did Ermengarde put that rat? Oh, for goodness sake! It was just a simple question! Stop screaming!'

Cook, despite an armchair and an eiderdown and hot-milk-with-brandy to settle her nerves, was wide awake and chattering.

'There she stood, in nothing but that nightdress! "My dear, dear, Amelia!" he says . . . He'll have to marry her now . . .'

Even Miss Minchin had words she must say.

'Amelia.'

'Maria?'

'I hope you will be very happy.'

'Oh, Maria!'

Eventually, however, they all became silent.

Lottie closed her eyes and was quiet. Gertrude and her companions settled down at last. Cook dozed and Alice snored. The Miss Minchins whispered, 'Goodnight, my dear,' 'Goodnight, my dear,' and fell asleep.

But in two little rooms at the top of the house Jessica and Lavinia and Ermengarde and Sara talked nearly till dawn.

* * *

'Oh, Sara! I thought you would go away to India and I would never see you again.'

'I thought you didn't want to, Ermie.'

'You didn't say in your letter you would be staying here tonight.'

'No. I didn't plan it. It was Mrs Carmichael's idea. Just in case you came back in the morning. I hoped and hoped you'd come back. Oh, Ermengarde, can you believe there is no more Miss Minchin's?'

'Yes I can,' said Ermengarde, sombrely. 'I can, because it is my fault. I wished it. It was my birthday wish. *No more Miss Minchin's.*'

Ermengarde paused, waiting for Sara to say, 'Don't be silly, Ermengarde!'

But Sara did not do that. Instead, she murmured, 'Poor Ermie,' and then sat thinking, her small dark head bowed, her thin brown hands clasped around her knees.

In the room next door Jessica was feeling rather wistful.

'I can't bear it,' she said sadly. 'It's all over! After all the lovely times we had . . .'

'Lovely times?' asked Lavinia, truly astonished.

'The stories by the schoolroom fire. Teaching you to

play the piano. Rushing for the post in the morning. Alice and her Epping, and the little ones in church. The cosy feeling of watching the rain from the windows when you were safe inside . . .'

'Ermengarde,' said Sara, raising her eyes at last, 'why did you wish for no more Miss Minchin's? Because you were unhappy?'

'I suppose,' admitted Ermengarde.

'Well, it wasn't your fault you were unhappy,' said Sara, 'and it isn't your fault that Miss Minchin's has gone. But I wish it hadn't. Oh, Ermie, do you remember the fairy stories we used to read when we were little? There was one where the children turned back in time. Wouldn't it be lovely if we could do that?'

'You would go back to Miss Minchin's?' asked Ermengarde incredulously.

'Yes I would. Just once. And I would take you, too. Back to the night of the banquet.'

'The night of the banquet?' repeated Ermengarde.

'Yes. Oh, Ermie, I wish I had shown you! I have wished it ever since. That was the night the magic came.'

'Tell me,' said Ermengarde.

'I fell asleep, and when I woke the attic had become beautiful. There were books and flowers, and a fire . . . There were so many things . . .'

Sara paused, remembering.

'For the first few days I could hardly believe it was real. And then I thought that perhaps it had just been lent, for the most dreadful times, do you understand?'

'Yes.'

'I knew I could trust *you*, Ermengarde, but for days and days I didn't trust *it*. And when those clothes came, do you remember? I began to feel like a person in a dream.'

'I would have, too,' said Ermengarde. 'I know I would have been just the same.'

'And then the monkey escaped from next door and came over the roof, and I took him back home to the Indian gentleman. And I found out that the Indian gentleman was Uncle Tom, and that he had been searching for me for years. And then I knew that nothing would ever be the same again. But I wish you had seen the magic, just once.'

'I did,' said Ermengarde. 'Just once. And now I'll tell you everything. Even about Lavinia.'

'Lavinia?'

'I cut off a curl of her hair,' said Ermengarde, and began to laugh.

From the bed beside her own Lavinia heard a sniff.

And then another.

'You're not crying are you, Jess?' she asked.

'Well, of course I am!' snuffled Jessica, a little indignantly.

'But why?'

'Because it's all gone! Miss Minchin's! It's all burned away. And the roof fell in. And if it wasn't for you we'd all be burned too . . .'

'Oh shut up, Jess!' said Lavinia, sharply.

'Sara,' said Ermengarde suddenly out of the darkness. 'About Melchisedec!'

'Goodness, Ermie! I forgot him! Where is he now?'

'In a box in the kitchen. And Sara, I've worked out what to do with him.'

'Have you really?'

'I'm going to give him to Aunt Eliza! That is, unless you want to take him to India with you? But I don't suppose that would be very easy.'

'I don't suppose it would. But do you think your Aunt Eliza will mind, Ermie?'

'She will have to put up with it,' said Ermengarde stolidly. 'She has put up with much worse! You would understand if you had ever met Uncle Julius. Anyway, Melchisedec has to live somewhere.'

'You all have to live somewhere,' said Sara, worriedly.

'I'm thinking about that,' replied Ermengarde.

Jessica would not shut up. She said, 'You saved us all, Lavinia. You know you did.'

'I didn't actually. I didn't save Ermengarde. That was Tristram.'

The roof had gone below the three of them at that final crossing. Dissolved into holes. Wooden struts had appeared and vanished at a clutch, tiles fell in cascades and sailed over the edge, billows of plaster dust blinded their eyes. The stocking rope saved Lavinia; it guided her to safety across the last few yards, but she lost her hold on Ermengarde. For just a moment though, she caught a glimpse of Tristram, swimming upwards through falling tiles with one hand, gripping

Ermengarde with the other.

She had thought she was seeing them both for the last time.

The horror was with her still, the falling and the noise, and the terrible helpless fear. Her heart raced, living it again.

'Tell me what actually happened, Lavinia,' persisted Jessica.

'I can't. I don't want to think about it. Go to sleep. If you don't, you won't be able to concentrate in the morning.'

'Concentrate on *what*?'

Lavinia did not answer. She breathed as if she were asleep. Under the pillow her fingers sought out her *Elementary Greek Grammar*. She began to recite in her head:

Alpha, beta, gamma, delta, epsilon . . .

The pounding in her heart began to lessen, and the picture of Ermengarde and Tristram to fade.

Zeta, eta, theta. Iota . . .

Jessica tried another subject.

'Miss Minchin's face afterwards when she saw Sara!'

. . . Kappa.

'But I can't understand why she said what she did. Sara, I mean.'

...*Lambda. Mu, nu, xi*...

'Why on earth should Sara say sorry to Miss Minchin?'

...*Omicron, pi, rho, sigma*...

'Lavinia, I don't believe you are really asleep.'

...*Tau. Upsilon. Phi*...

'Oh well.'

...*Chi*...

'Goodnight. It must be very nearly morning.'

...*Psi*...

'You were wonderful, Lavinia.'

Omega.

Sounds Like a Storybook

LONG AGO, WHEN MISS MINCHIN HAD
first dreamed the Select Seminary into existence, she had
known the sort of parents she wished to attract.

'Detached,' she had decided, meaning those who were
uninterested, abroad, very ill, or (most uncritical and
remote of all) dead. And by offering provision for
holidays she had succeeded in attracting these most
desirable fee payers.

In consequence, when the Select Seminary was burned
to the ground and the explaining telegrams sent off to
those who might be concerned, there was no rush of
anxious relations and guardians to reclaim the Young
Ladies. Jessica's parents were the only ones who actually

turned up, and they were received with wails of dismay from their daughter, who was having far too interesting a time to think of coming home. In the end they went away empty-handed, but at least they had tried. The rest sent polite variations of the words, '*So pleased to hear . . . is safe. Please forward new address at your convenience.*'

'Aunt Eliza,' said Ermengarde. 'You have a large empty house, and Melchisedec is there already . . .'

And so in the end, wrote Ermengarde to Sara, *we nearly all came here. To Aunt Eliza's. She has turned her home into a boarding house, and every day, guess what, we all go to school by train! It is only a twelve-minute journey, and such fun. But the homework is dreadful and we cannot get Lavinia to help us with it in the evenings very much, and I will tell you how that has happened.*

Oh, Sara, I never thought I would feel sorry for Miss Minchin, but on the day we all met in Mrs Carmichael's drawing room to find out what was going to happen to us, I truly did. Because there was Miss Amelia waggling the vicar's diamond to catch the light, and Tristram's uncle telling about the school Tristram's sisters went to, and how good it was, and how we could easily travel there by train, and Aunt Eliza saying, 'Oh how wonderful to have a house full of girls!' And all the while Miss Minchin sat very quietly with one hand on her forehead and the other holding her locket.

And nobody asked what she thought about anything. Nobody needed to. She didn't seem to matter any more.

I was very sorry for her indeed, but I did not have any idea of what to do to help.

Lavinia did though.

Lavinia said in her coldest, most Lavinia-ish voice, 'But what about me? This new school sounds all very well . . .' (she did not look at Tristram's uncle when she said that, nor show any sign of having read the prospectus so often that it did not matter that it had been burned in the fire because she could recite it anyway) '. . . and I am very glad to be going there. But I was making a special study of English literature with Miss Minchin and what will happen about that? I hope I can still continue?'

'Why, Lavinia dear,' said Miss Amelia. 'I don't know. It may not be possible. The vicarage is quite some distance . . .'

'But I shall not need to go the vicarage, shall I?' asked Lavinia. 'Now that Miss Minchin is free at last . . .' (we all saw the tiny glance she gave at Miss Amelia's diamond, Sara!) 'to get on properly with her own work . . .'

(The whole room was staring at Lavinia by this time, but she did not seem to notice.)

'. . . her Shakespeare research,' she continued, 'and her writing . . .'

She looked across at Miss Minchin then, and Miss Minchin said, like a person waking up from a dream, 'Yes, of course, my research and my writing!' And her head was no longer in her hand.

'But will you do that at the vicarage, Miss Minchin?'

'Certainly not,' said Miss Minchin. 'There is no reason at all that I should. The Seminary was amply insured. My sister no longer needs my support. I have many times thought of buying a small house of my own . . .'

'But do you think you will still have time for private tutoring?' persisted Lavinia.

'Really!' exclaimed Miss Minchin, looking quite alive now. 'When have I ever neglected my duties to my pupils, may I ask?'

'So even if I have to live with Ermengarde's aunt . . .'

'As a matter of fact, Lavinia dear, I was about to suggest . . .'

'Oh!' exclaimed Lottie, interrupting all of a sudden. 'Oh, I know what you're going to say! You are going to let Lavvie stay with you! Oh, it's not fair! What if Ermengarde's aunt's house catches fire next? Who will get us out if Lavinia is with Miss Minchin?'

'Lottie, if you are going to make a scene I think you had better go outside,' said Lavinia severely.

'It's all very well for you! You are having the best of everything! You won't have to live in a house with a rat! Oh yes, don't shake your head at me like that, Lavinia! There is a rat; you ask Ermengarde! She knows! And so she should because it was she who let it loose in the attic! And I bet you still get to go to school by train, as well!'

'Yes, I expect I will,' said Lavinia calmly.

'*AND I suppose you will have a lovely room of your own.*'

'*Naturally Lavinia will have a room of her own,*' said Miss Minchin.

'*Well, I am not making a scene,*' said Lottie crossly. '*But it isn't fair. Not if I have to live in the rat house with all the boring little ones, and Lavinia is allowed to live with Miss Minchin AND go to school on the train AND have a room of her own JUST because she is Miss Minchin's favourite and has been at school since she was four. I have been at school since I was four, so what about me? I suppose Alice will be at Miss Minchin's too!*'

'*I'd like to know how she'd manage without me!*' said Alice, sniffing.

Then Lottie stamped out of the room and sulked on the stairs until she was given entirely her own way. As usual. But afterwards I saw Lavinia hugging her, and Tristram gave her Bosco to keep for ever. A reward for heroism, he said. Tristram's uncle said Lavinia deserved a reward too, and he took her to Oxford to meet Tristram's sisters. Lavinia came back sort of shining, Sara. Alice called it uppity.

And that is how Lottie and Lavinia and Bosco ended up living with Miss Minchin in a little house not far from Aunt Eliza's with Alice to look after them, and Cook to cook. Alice says they have Miss Minchin wound round their little fingers, but I think Miss Minchin likes being wound.

You only have to look at her to see she is happy.

She wears her gold locket all the time now.

'*She has got us inside,*' says Lottie smugly. '*Lavinia and*

Bosco and me all together. We had our photographs taken specially. Do you want to hear me say the alphabet in Greek?'

   'No thank you,' I say, but she does it anyway.

And that is all the news for now, and I will post this letter tomorrow, and soon it will be in India.

   I do like writing to you, Sara.

Sara, do you remember the day we first met? I was sitting on that deep window seat at Miss Minchin's and you came across the room and asked me my name. I was so flustered and pleased I could hardly speak, but I remember saying very carefully, 'My name is Ermengarde St John.'

And you said, 'Mine is Sara Crewe. Yours is very pretty.
It sounds like a storybook.'

A Catalogue record for this book is available from the British Library

ISBN-13: 978 0 340 95653 3

Typeset in Archetype by Avon DataSet Ltd,
Bidford on Avon, Warwickshire

Printed and bound in Great Britain by
Bookmarque Ltd, Croydon, Surrey

The paper used in this book is a natural recyclable product made
from wood grown in sustainable forests. The hard coverboard is recycled.

Hodder Children's Books
a division of Hachette Children's Books
338 Euston Road, London NW1 3BH
An Hachette UK Company
www.hachette.co.uk

THE CASSON FAMILY...

Meet **Rose, Indigo, Saffy** and **Caddy:**

Hilary McKay's Casson family are eccentric, artistic, and very, very real.

Also by Hilary McKay

THE CASSON FAMILY
Saffy's Angel
(Winner of the Whitbread Children's Book Award)
Indigo's Star
Permanent Rose
Caddy Ever After
Forever Rose

The Exiles
(Winner of the Guardian Book Award)
The Exiles at Home
(Winner of the Nestlé Smarties Prize)
The Exiles in Love

Dog Friday
Amber Cat
Dolphin Luck

FOR YOUNGER READERS:

The Story of Bear

Happy and Glorious
Practically Perfect

PARADISE HOUSE
The Treasure in the Garden
The Echo in the Chimney
The Zoo in the Attic
The Magic in the Mirror
The Surprise Party
Keeping Cottontail

PUDDING BAG SCHOOL
A Birthday Wish
Cold Enough for Snow
A Strong Smell of Magic